MARY SHELLEY'S

FRANKENSTEIN

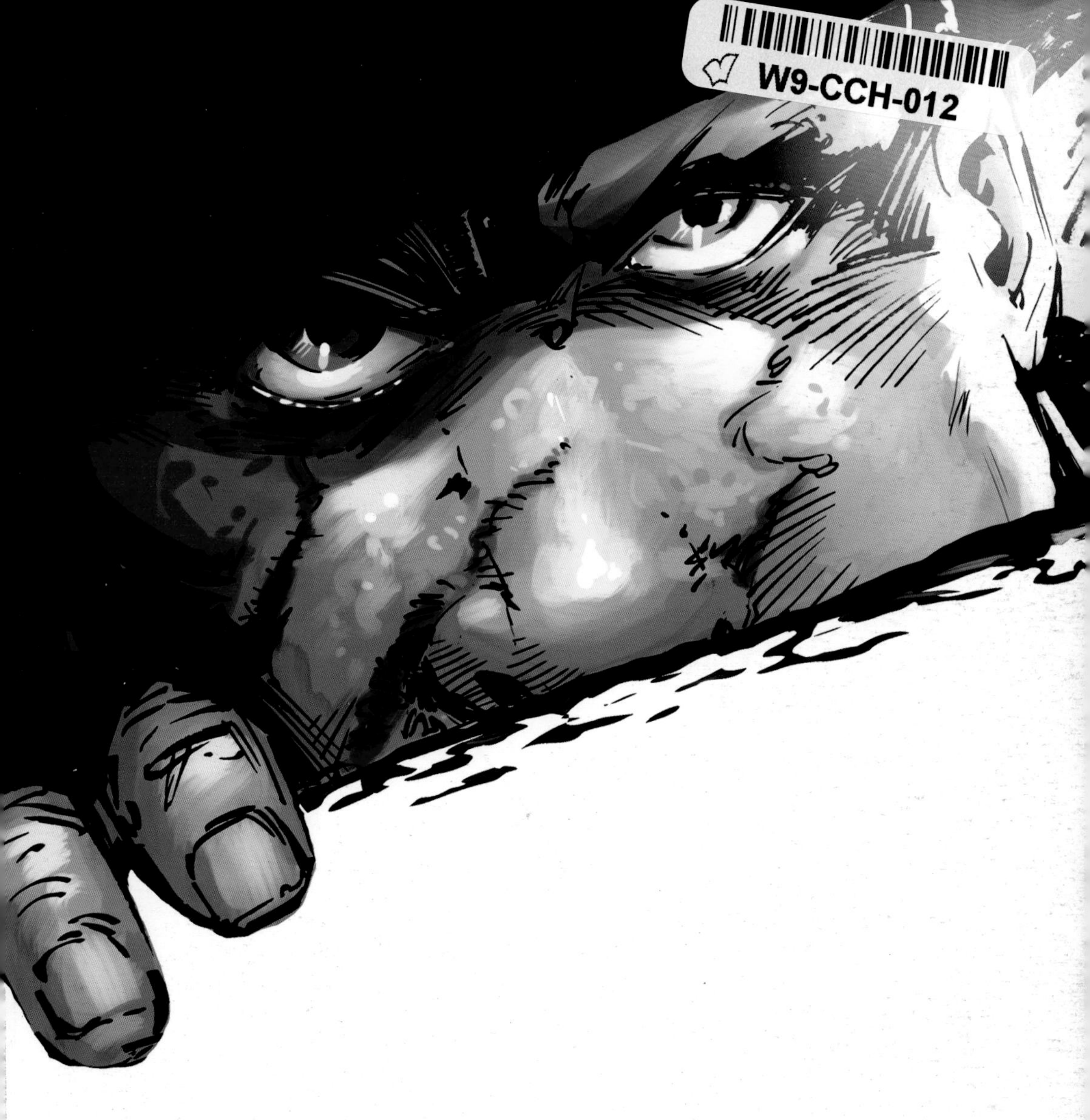

CAMPFIRE®

KALYANI NAVYUG MEDIA PVT LTD

Sitting around the Campfire, telling the story, were:

Wordsmith	:	Lloyd S. Wagner
Illustrator	:	Naresh Kumar
Colorist	:	Anil C. K.
Letterer	:	Bhavnath Chaudhary
Editors	:	Divya Dubey
		Eman Chowdhary
Designer	:	Mukesh Rawat
Cover Artists		
Illustrator	:	Naresh Kumar
Colorist/Designer	:	Jayakrishnan K. P.

CAMPFIRE®

www.campfire.co.in

MISSION STATEMENT
To entertain and educate young minds by creating unique illustrated books
that recount stories of human values, arouse curiosity in the world around us,
and inspire with tales of great deeds of unforgettable people.

Published by Kalyani Navyug Media Pvt Ltd
101 C, Shiv House, Hari Nagar Ashram
New Delhi 110014
India

ISBN: 978-93-80028-24-8

Printed in India

About the Author

Mary Wollstonecraft Shelley was born in London, England on August 30, 1797. She is best known for her novel *Frankenstein* which was published in 1818, when Shelley was only twenty years of age.

Shelley's interest in science fiction was influenced by her father, who was fascinated with developments in scientific thinking during the nineteenth century. This interest was followed by Shelley who would regularly attend science lectures in London.

When she was sixteen years old, Shelley met and fell in love with the poet Percy Bysshe Shelley. They seemed to be the perfect match of literary pursuits, and Percy was pleased with their shared interest in poetry. They married in 1816.

Percy influenced his wife's writing with his interest in radical science. Shelley's ideas for *Frankenstein* had the weight of personal interest and research into the subject of galvanism, and beliefs that a corpse could be brought back to life using electricity.

It was this interest in science and a love of ghost stories that motivated Shelley to create her macabre tale. In the introduction to her novel, Shelley also admitted to a desire to frighten her readers.

Frankenstein was a great success in its initial publication, and Shelley revised the story in its later printing. Despite the novel's success, Shelley would live in the shadow of her more famous husband. When Percy died in 1822, Shelley devoted herself to publicizing her husband's work.

Shelley's later novels never gripped the public's attention as *Frankenstein* had; the novel continues to intrigue modern readers, and has been the subject of several books and films.

Mary Wollstonecraft Shelley died of a suspected brain tumor on February 1, 1851.

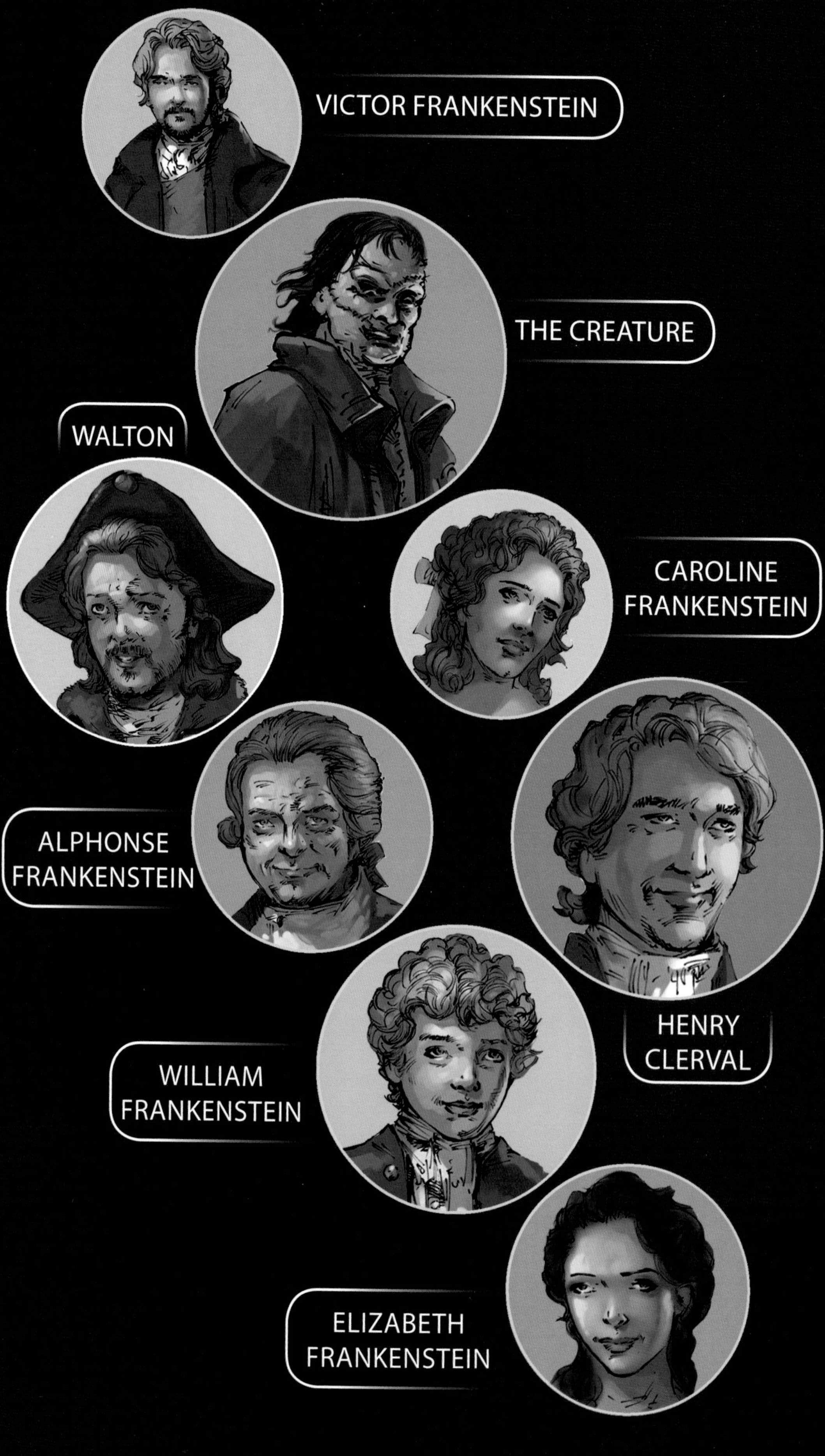
VICTOR FRANKENSTEIN
THE CREATURE
WALTON
CAROLINE FRANKENSTEIN
ALPHONSE FRANKENSTEIN
HENRY CLERVAL
WILLIAM FRANKENSTEIN
ELIZABETH FRANKENSTEIN

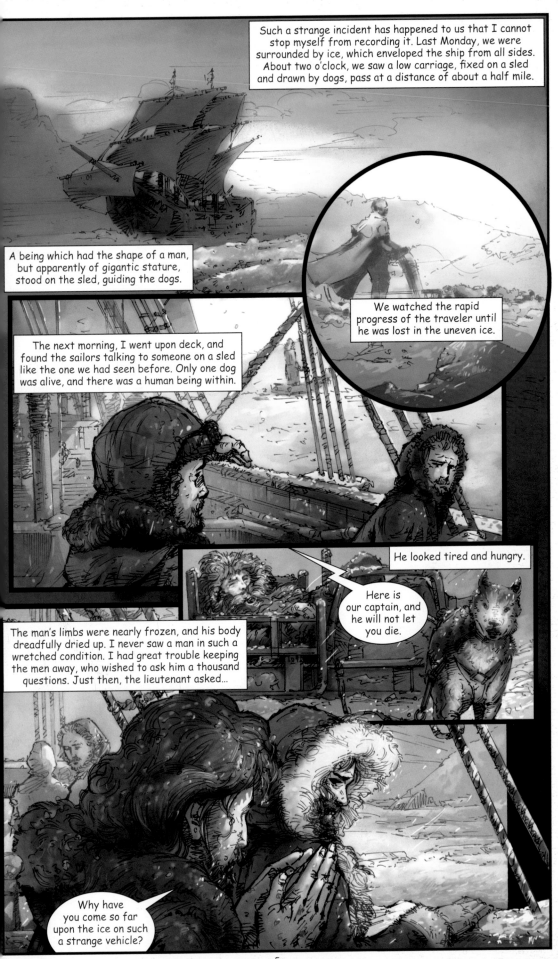

Such a strange incident has happened to us that I cannot stop myself from recording it. Last Monday, we were surrounded by ice, which enveloped the ship from all sides. About two o'clock, we saw a low carriage, fixed on a sled and drawn by dogs, pass at a distance of about a half mile.

A being which had the shape of a man, but apparently of gigantic stature, stood on the sled, guiding the dogs.

We watched the rapid progress of the traveler until he was lost in the uneven ice.

The next morning, I went upon deck, and found the sailors talking to someone on a sled like the one we had seen before. Only one dog was alive, and there was a human being within.

He looked tired and hungry.

Here is our captain, and he will not let you die.

The man's limbs were nearly frozen, and his body dreadfully dried up. I never saw a man in such a wretched condition. I had great trouble keeping the men away, who wished to ask him a thousand questions. Just then, the lieutenant asked...

Why have you come so far upon the ice on such a strange vehicle?

5

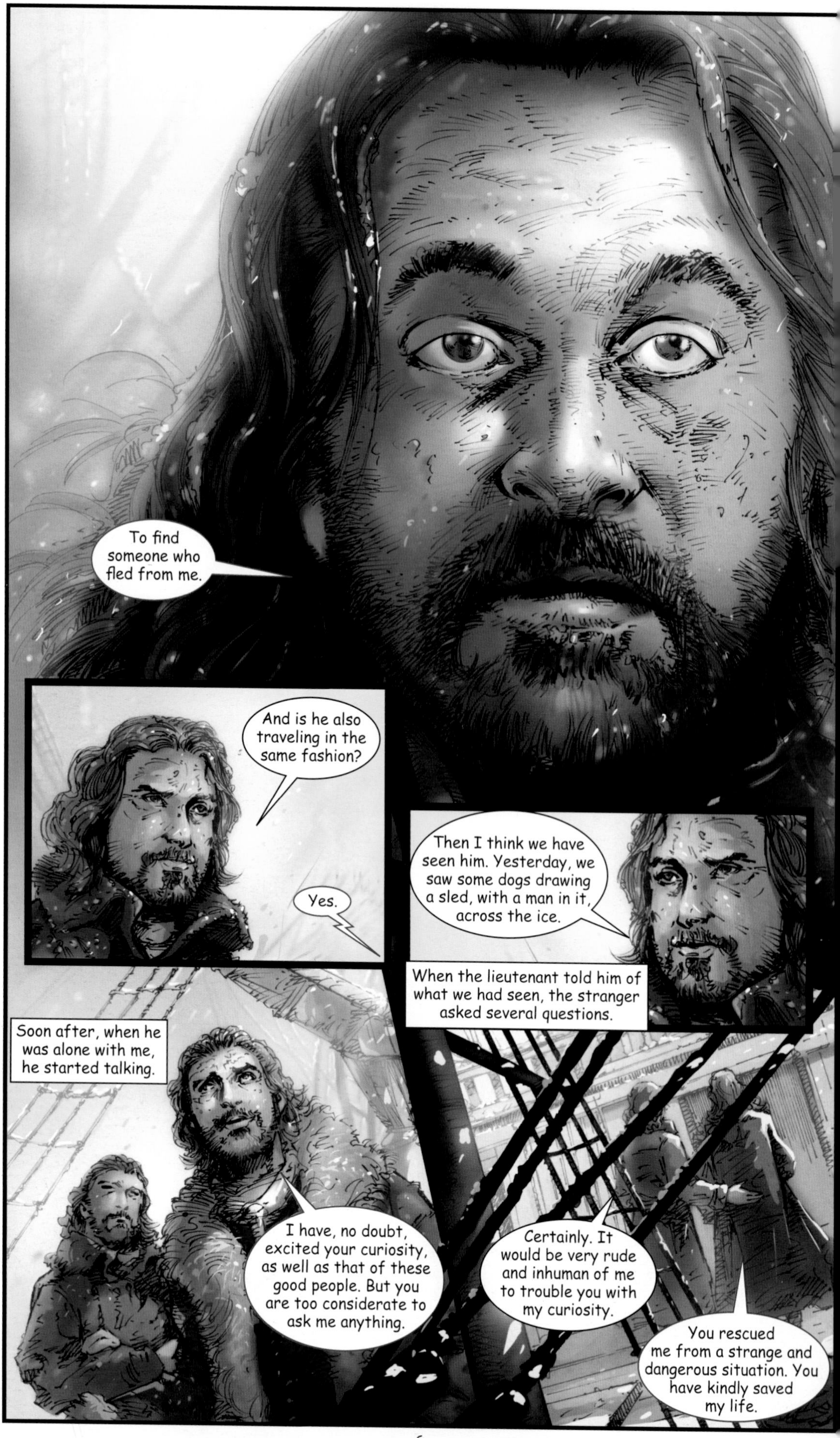
To find someone who fled from me.
And is he also traveling in the same fashion?
Yes.
When the lieutenant told him of what we had seen, the stranger asked several questions.
Then I think we have seen him. Yesterday, we saw some dogs drawing a sled, with a man in it, across the ice.
Soon after, when he was alone with me, he started talking.
I have, no doubt, excited your curiosity, as well as that of these good people. But you are too considerate to ask me anything.
Certainly. It would be very rude and inhuman of me to trouble you with my curiosity.
You rescued me from a strange and dangerous situation. You have kindly saved my life.

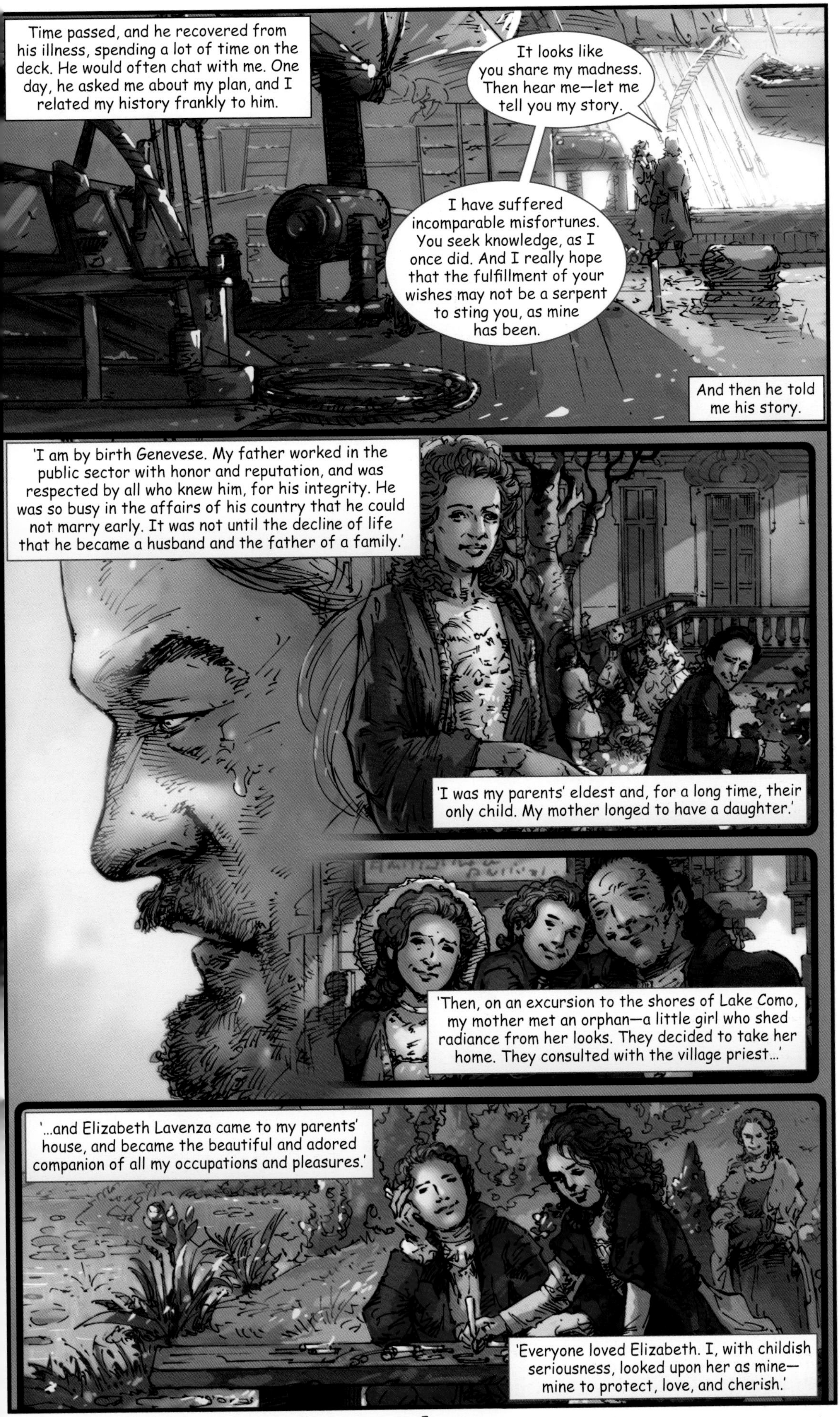
Time passed, and he recovered from his illness, spending a lot of time on the deck. He would often chat with me. One day, he asked me about my plan, and I related my history frankly to him.
It looks like you share my madness. Then hear me—let me tell you my story.
I have suffered incomparable misfortunes. You seek knowledge, as I once did. And I really hope that the fulfillment of your wishes may not be a serpent to sting you, as mine has been.
And then he told me his story.
'I am by birth Genevese. My father worked in the public sector with honor and reputation, and was respected by all who knew him, for his integrity. He was so busy in the affairs of his country that he could not marry early. It was not until the decline of life that he became a husband and the father of a family.'
'I was my parents' eldest and, for a long time, their only child. My mother longed to have a daughter.'
'Then, on an excursion to the shores of Lake Como, my mother met an orphan—a little girl who shed radiance from her looks. They decided to take her home. They consulted with the village priest...'
'...and Elizabeth Lavenza came to my parents' house, and became the beautiful and adored companion of all my occupations and pleasures.'
'Everyone loved Elizabeth. I, with childish seriousness, looked upon her as mine—mine to protect, love, and cherish.'

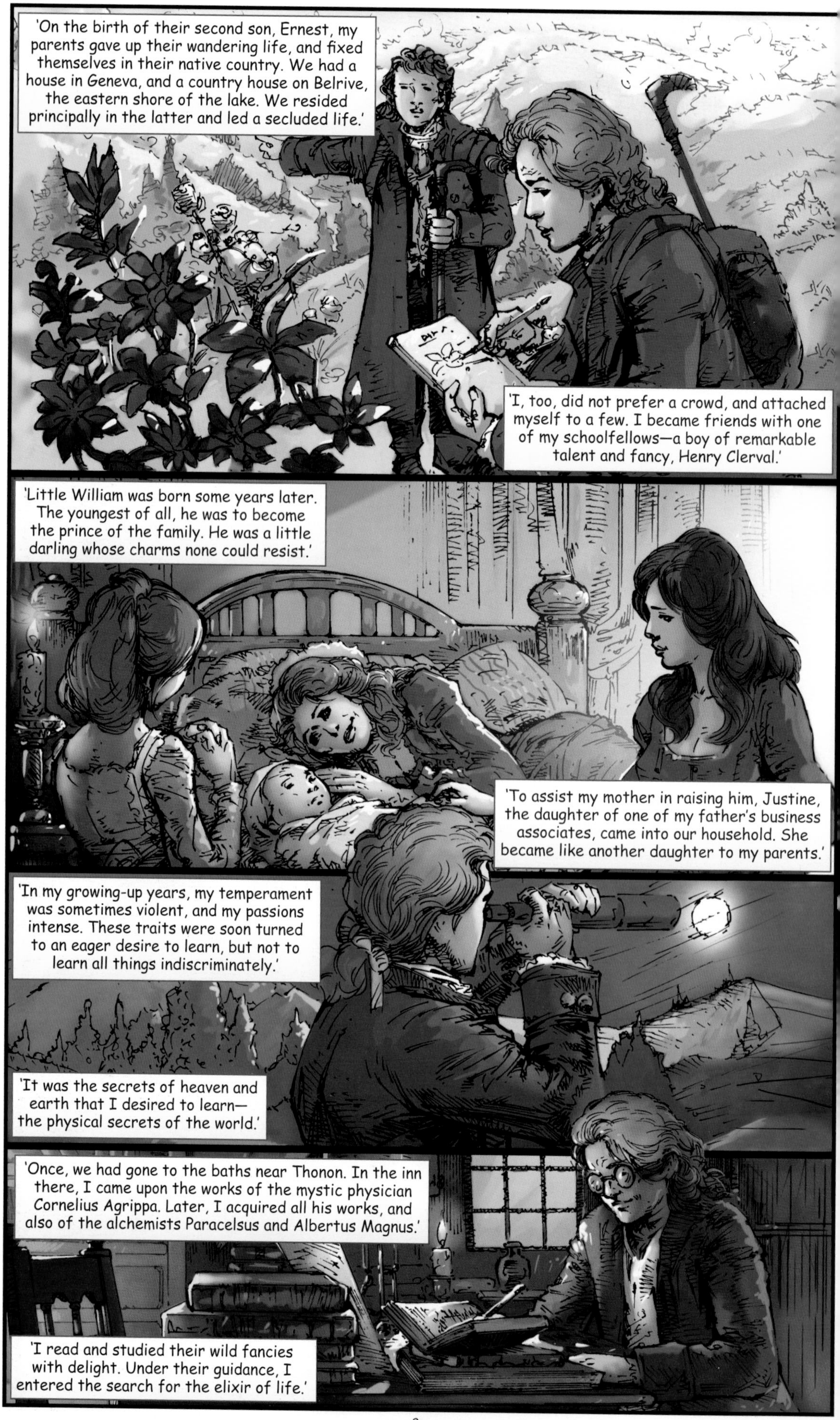
'On the birth of their second son, Ernest, my parents gave up their wandering life, and fixed themselves in their native country. We had a house in Geneva, and a country house on Belrive, the eastern shore of the lake. We resided principally in the latter and led a secluded life.'
'I, too, did not prefer a crowd, and attached myself to a few. I became friends with one of my schoolfellows—a boy of remarkable talent and fancy, Henry Clerval.'
'Little William was born some years later. The youngest of all, he was to become the prince of the family. He was a little darling whose charms none could resist.'
'To assist my mother in raising him, Justine, the daughter of one of my father's business associates, came into our household. She became like another daughter to my parents.'
'In my growing-up years, my temperament was sometimes violent, and my passions intense. These traits were soon turned to an eager desire to learn, but not to learn all things indiscriminately.'
'It was the secrets of heaven and earth that I desired to learn—the physical secrets of the world.'
'Once, we had gone to the baths near Thonon. In the inn there, I came upon the works of the mystic physician Cornelius Agrippa. Later, I acquired all his works, and also of the alchemists Paracelsus and Albertus Magnus.'
'I read and studied their wild fancies with delight. Under their guidance, I entered the search for the elixir of life.'

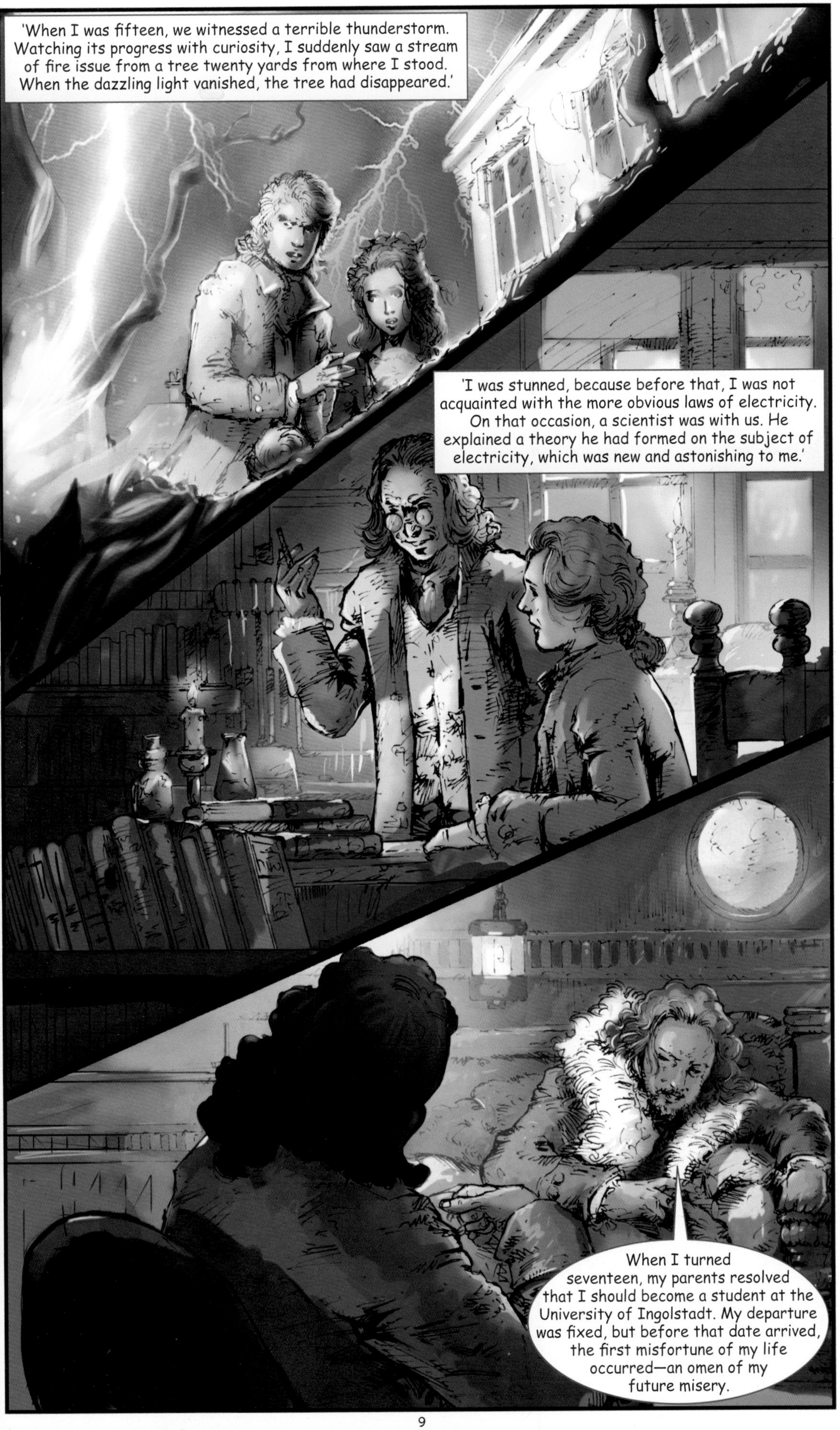
'When I was fifteen, we witnessed a terrible thunderstorm. Watching its progress with curiosity, I suddenly saw a stream of fire issue from a tree twenty yards from where I stood. When the dazzling light vanished, the tree had disappeared.'
'I was stunned, because before that, I was not acquainted with the more obvious laws of electricity. On that occasion, a scientist was with us. He explained a theory he had formed on the subject of electricity, which was new and astonishing to me.'
When I turned seventeen, my parents resolved that I should become a student at the University of Ingolstadt. My departure was fixed, but before that date arrived, the first misfortune of my life occurred—an omen of my future misery.

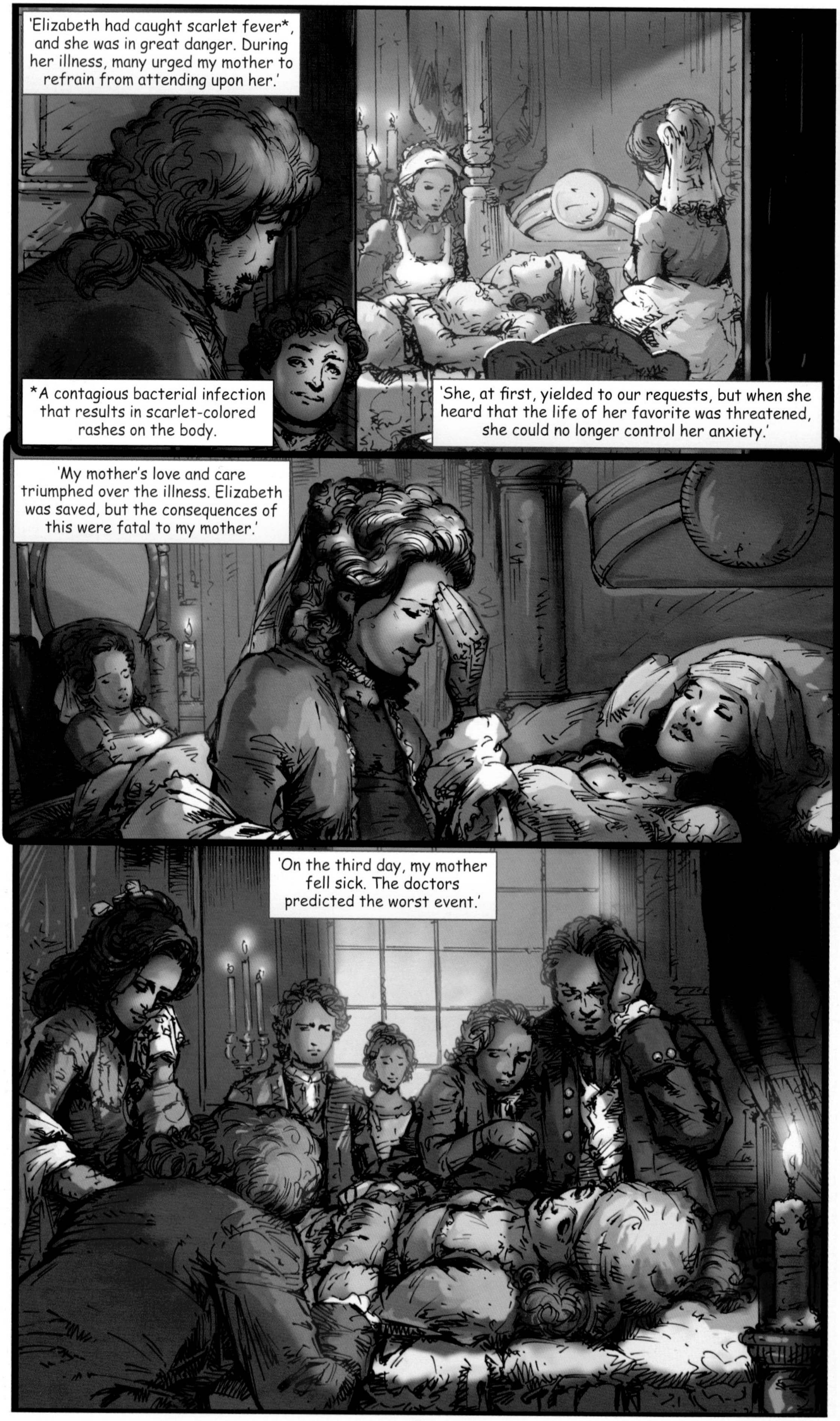
'Elizabeth had caught scarlet fever*, and she was in great danger. During her illness, many urged my mother to refrain from attending upon her.'
*A contagious bacterial infection that results in scarlet-colored rashes on the body.
'She, at first, yielded to our requests, but when she heard that the life of her favorite was threatened, she could no longer control her anxiety.'
'My mother's love and care triumphed over the illness. Elizabeth was saved, but the consequences of this were fatal to my mother.'
'On the third day, my mother fell sick. The doctors predicted the worst event.'

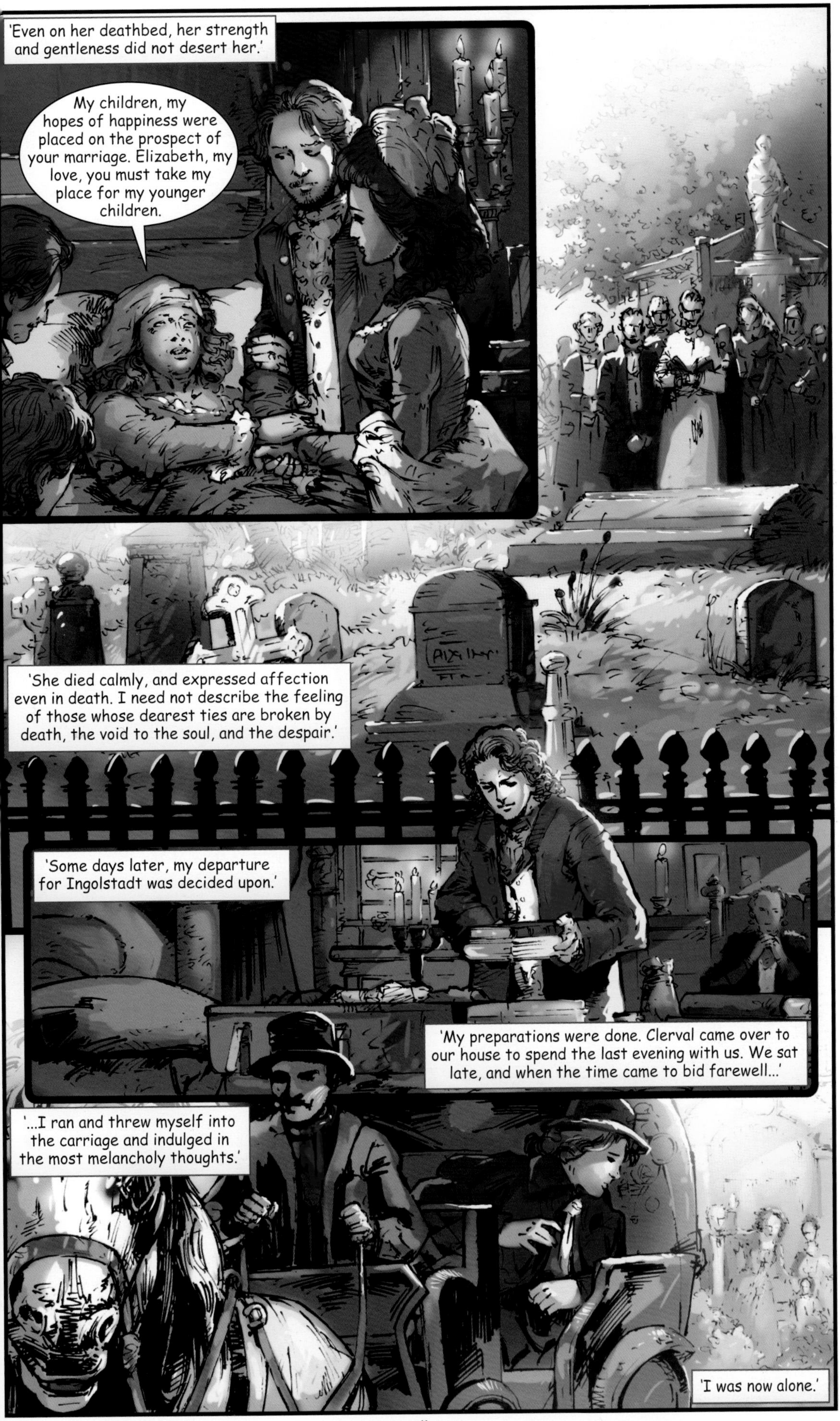
'Even on her deathbed, her strength and gentleness did not desert her.'
My children, my hopes of happiness were placed on the prospect of your marriage. Elizabeth, my love, you must take my place for my younger children.
'She died calmly, and expressed affection even in death. I need not describe the feeling of those whose dearest ties are broken by death, the void to the soul, and the despair.'
'Some days later, my departure for Ingolstadt was decided upon.'
'My preparations were done. Clerval came over to our house to spend the last evening with us. We sat late, and when the time came to bid farewell...'
'...I ran and threw myself into the carriage and indulged in the most melancholy thoughts.'
'I was now alone.'

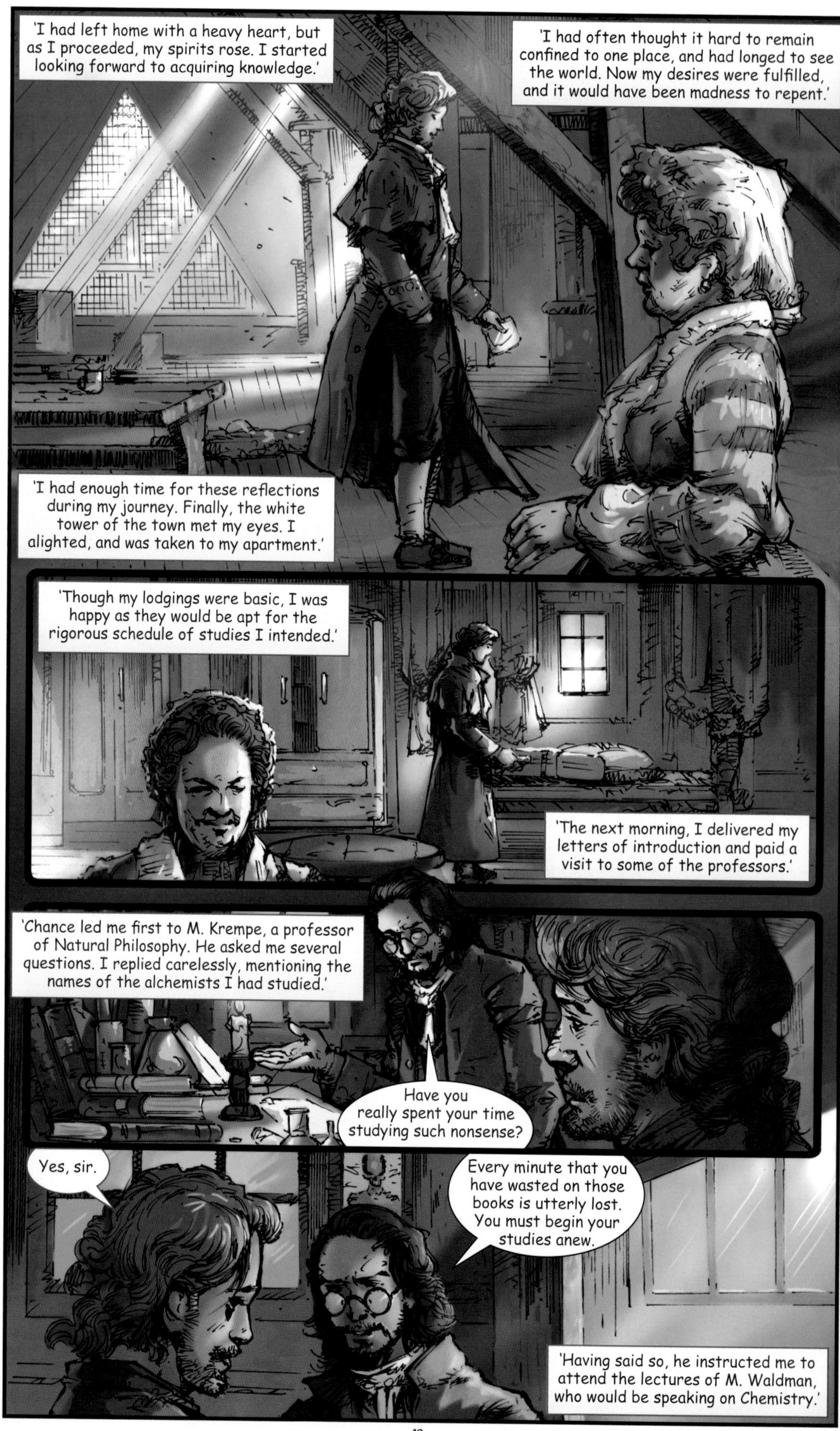
'I had left home with a heavy heart, but as I proceeded, my spirits rose. I started looking forward to acquiring knowledge.'
'I had often thought it hard to remain confined to one place, and had longed to see the world. Now my desires were fulfilled, and it would have been madness to repent.'
'I had enough time for these reflections during my journey. Finally, the white tower of the town met my eyes. I alighted, and was taken to my apartment.'
'Though my lodgings were basic, I was happy as they would be apt for the rigorous schedule of studies I intended.'
'The next morning, I delivered my letters of introduction and paid a visit to some of the professors.'
'Chance led me first to M. Krempe, a professor of Natural Philosophy. He asked me several questions. I replied carelessly, mentioning the names of the alchemists I had studied.'
Have you really spent your time studying such nonsense?
Yes, sir.
Every minute that you have wasted on those books is utterly lost. You must begin your studies anew.
'Having said so, he instructed me to attend the lectures of M. Waldman, who would be speaking on Chemistry.'

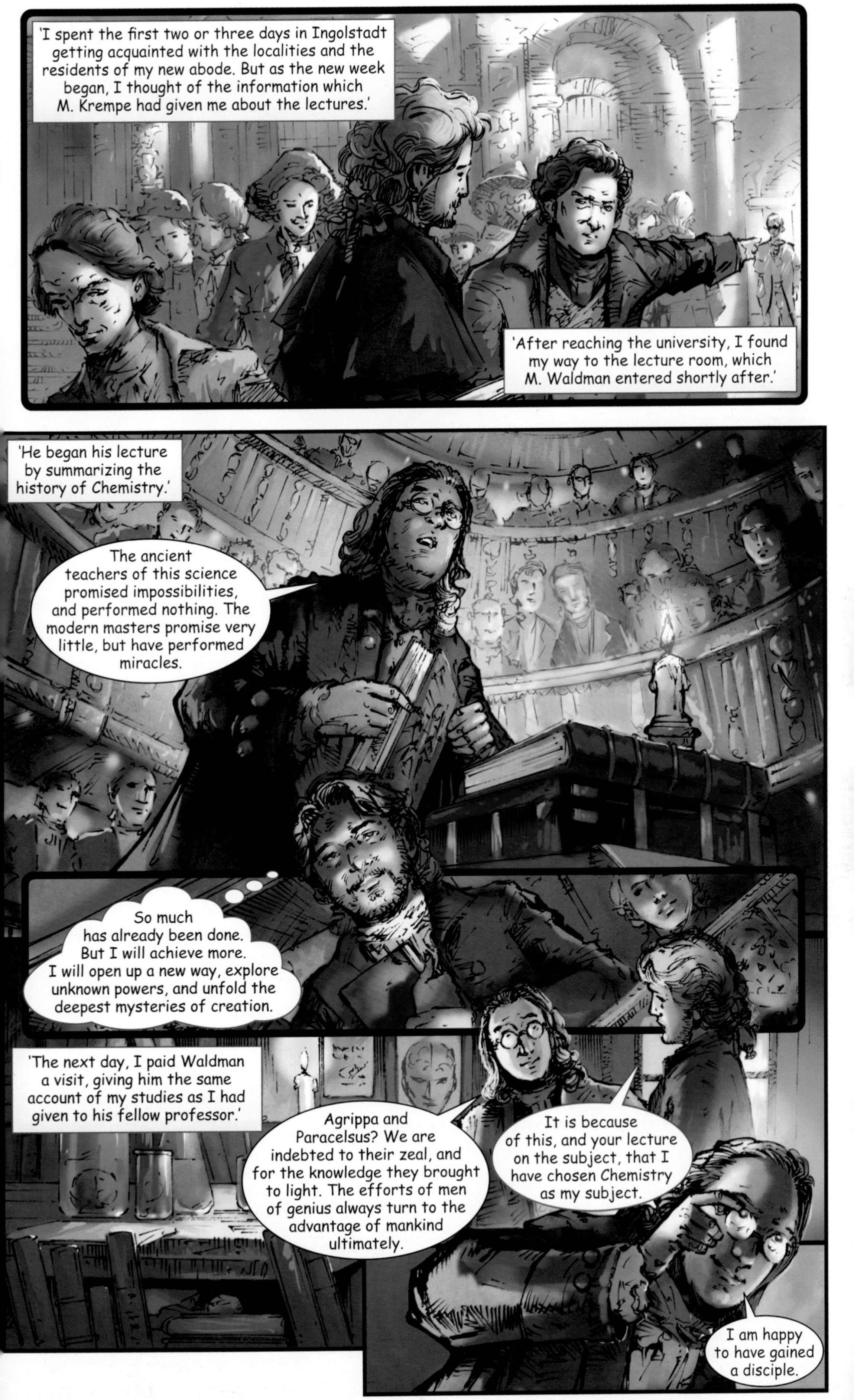
'I spent the first two or three days in Ingolstadt getting acquainted with the localities and the residents of my new abode. But as the new week began, I thought of the information which M. Krempe had given me about the lectures.'
'After reaching the university, I found my way to the lecture room, which M. Waldman entered shortly after.'
'He began his lecture by summarizing the history of Chemistry.'
The ancient teachers of this science promised impossibilities, and performed nothing. The modern masters promise very little, but have performed miracles.
So much has already been done. But I will achieve more. I will open up a new way, explore unknown powers, and unfold the deepest mysteries of creation.
'The next day, I paid Waldman a visit, giving him the same account of my studies as I had given to his fellow professor.'
Agrippa and Paracelsus? We are indebted to their zeal, and for the knowledge they brought to light. The efforts of men of genius always turn to the advantage of mankind ultimately.
It is because of this, and your lecture on the subject, that I have chosen Chemistry as my subject.
I am happy to have gained a disciple.

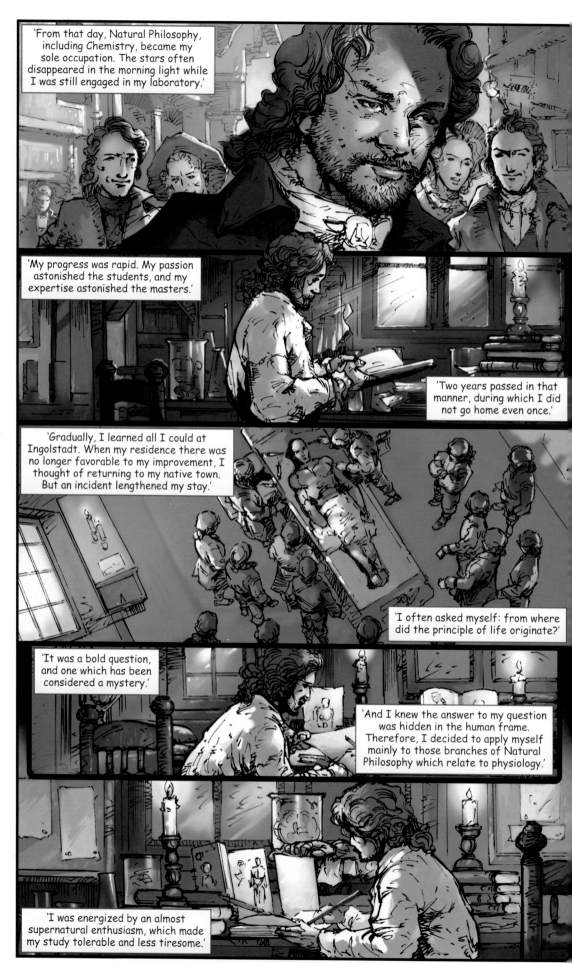

'From that day, Natural Philosophy, including Chemistry, became my sole occupation. The stars often disappeared in the morning light while I was still engaged in my laboratory.'

'My progress was rapid. My passion astonished the students, and my expertise astonished the masters.'

'Two years passed in that manner, during which I did not go home even once.'

'Gradually, I learned all I could at Ingolstadt. When my residence there was no longer favorable to my improvement, I thought of returning to my native town. But an incident lengthened my stay.'

'I often asked myself: from where did the principle of life originate?'

'It was a bold question, and one which has been considered a mystery.'

'And I knew the answer to my question was hidden in the human frame. Therefore, I decided to apply myself mainly to those branches of Natural Philosophy which relate to physiology.'

'I was energized by an almost supernatural enthusiasm, which made my study tolerable and less tiresome.'

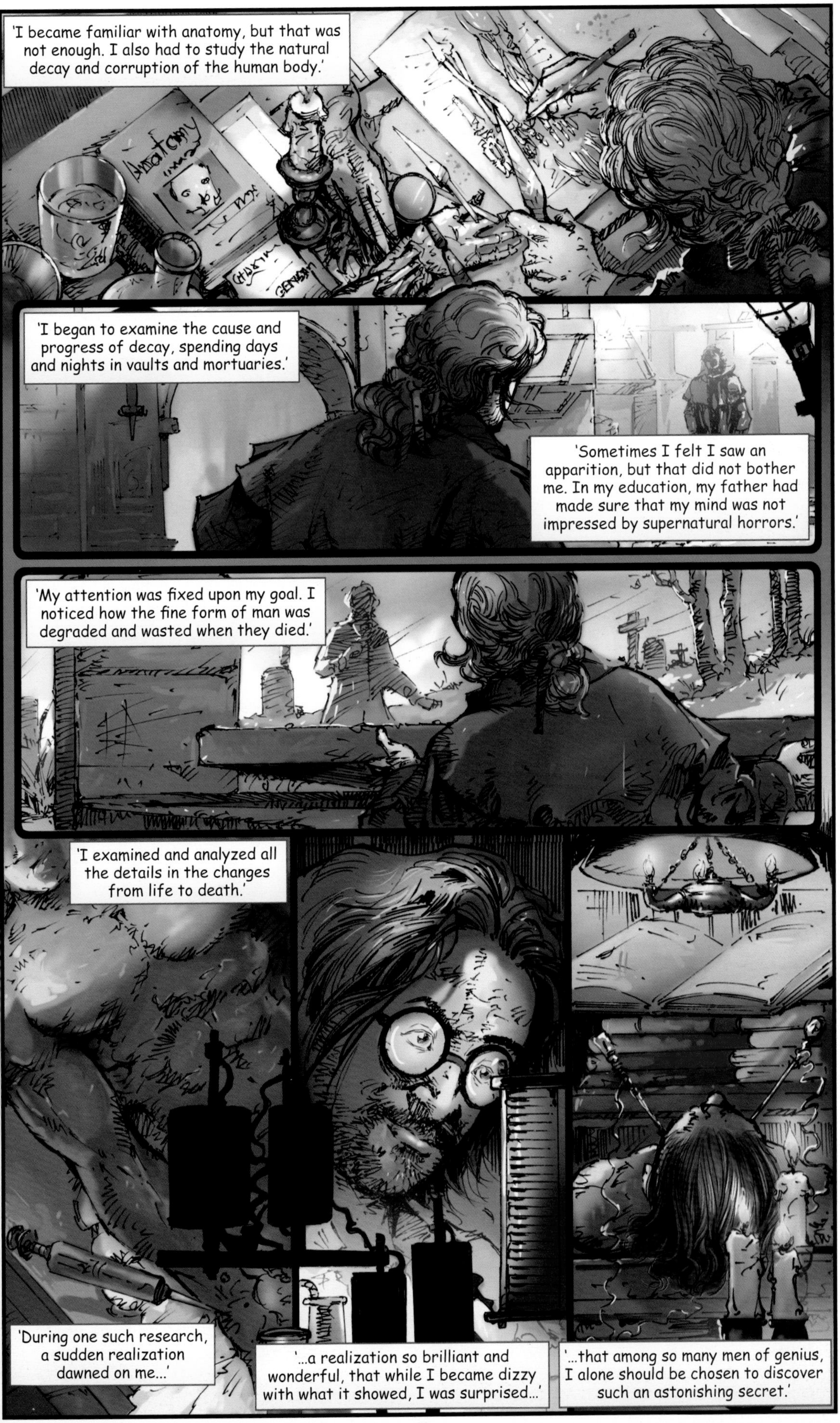
'I became familiar with anatomy, but that was not enough. I also had to study the natural decay and corruption of the human body.'
'I began to examine the cause and progress of decay, spending days and nights in vaults and mortuaries.'
'Sometimes I felt I saw an apparition, but that did not bother me. In my education, my father had made sure that my mind was not impressed by supernatural horrors.'
'My attention was fixed upon my goal. I noticed how the fine form of man was degraded and wasted when they died.'
'I examined and analyzed all the details in the changes from life to death.'
'During one such research, a sudden realization dawned on me...'
'...a realization so brilliant and wonderful, that while I became dizzy with what it showed, I was surprised...'
'...that among so many men of genius, I alone should be chosen to discover such an astonishing secret.'

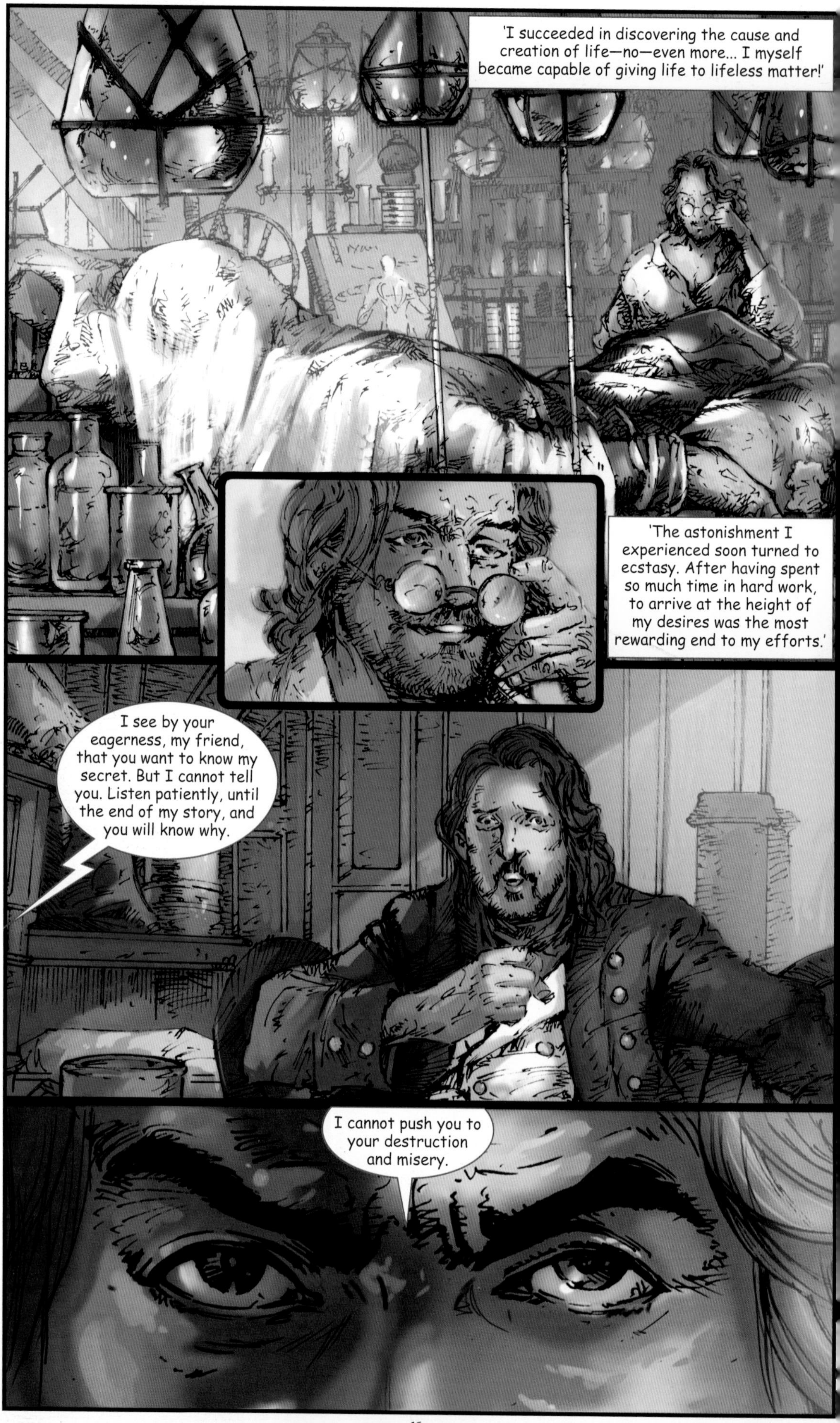
'I succeeded in discovering the cause and creation of life—no—even more... I myself became capable of giving life to lifeless matter!'
'The astonishment I experienced soon turned to ecstasy. After having spent so much time in hard work, to arrive at the height of my desires was the most rewarding end to my efforts.'
I see by your eagerness, my friend, that you want to know my secret. But I cannot tell you. Listen patiently, until the end of my story, and you will know why.
I cannot push you to your destruction and misery.

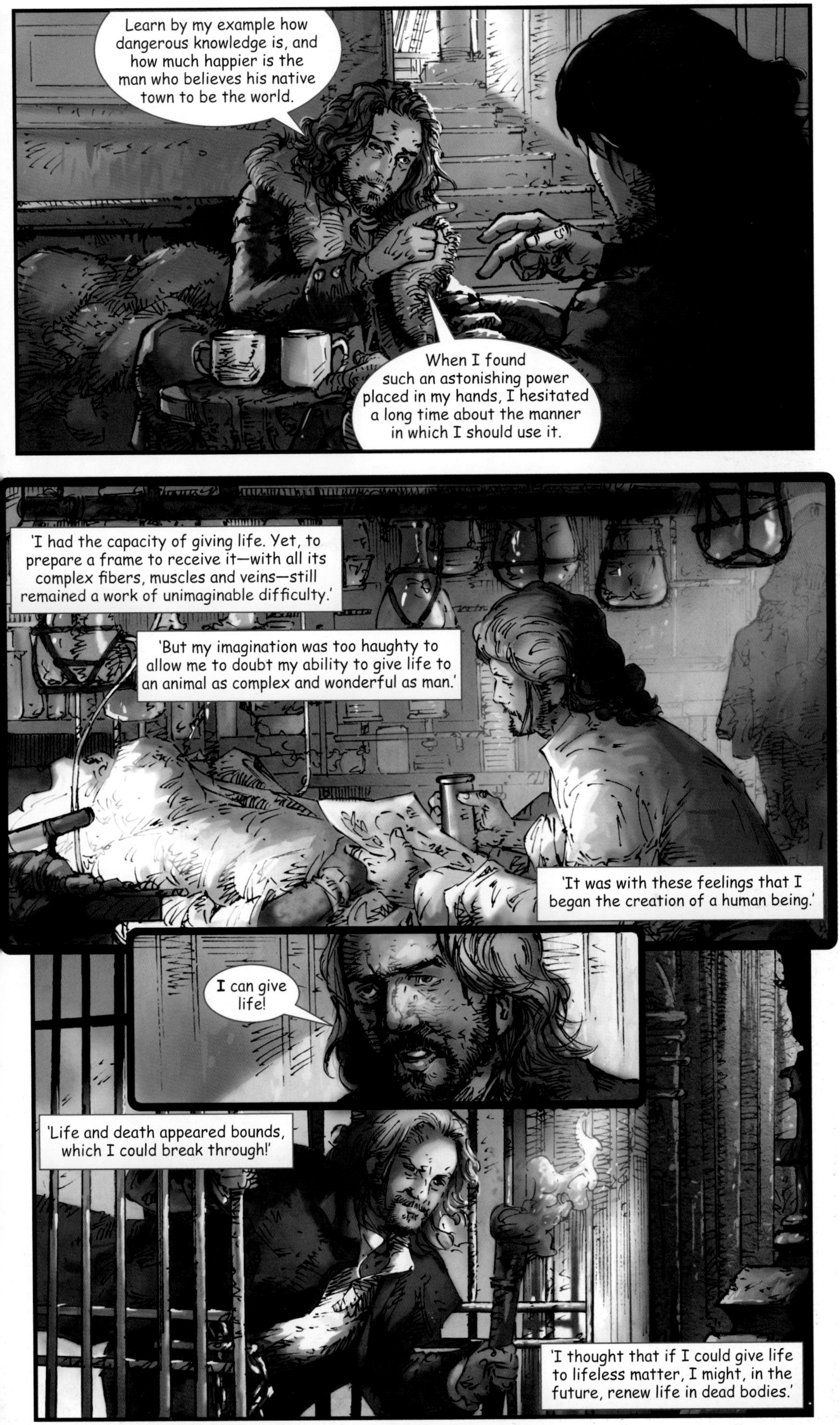
Learn by my example how dangerous knowledge is, and how much happier is the man who believes his native town to be the world.
When I found such an astonishing power placed in my hands, I hesitated a long time about the manner in which I should use it.
'I had the capacity of giving life. Yet, to prepare a frame to receive it—with all its complex fibers, muscles and veins—still remained a work of unimaginable difficulty.'
'But my imagination was too haughty to allow me to doubt my ability to give life to an animal as complex and wonderful as man.'
'It was with these feelings that I began the creation of a human being.'
I can give life!
'Life and death appeared bounds, which I could break through!'
'I thought that if I could give life to lifeless matter, I might, in the future, renew life in dead bodies.'

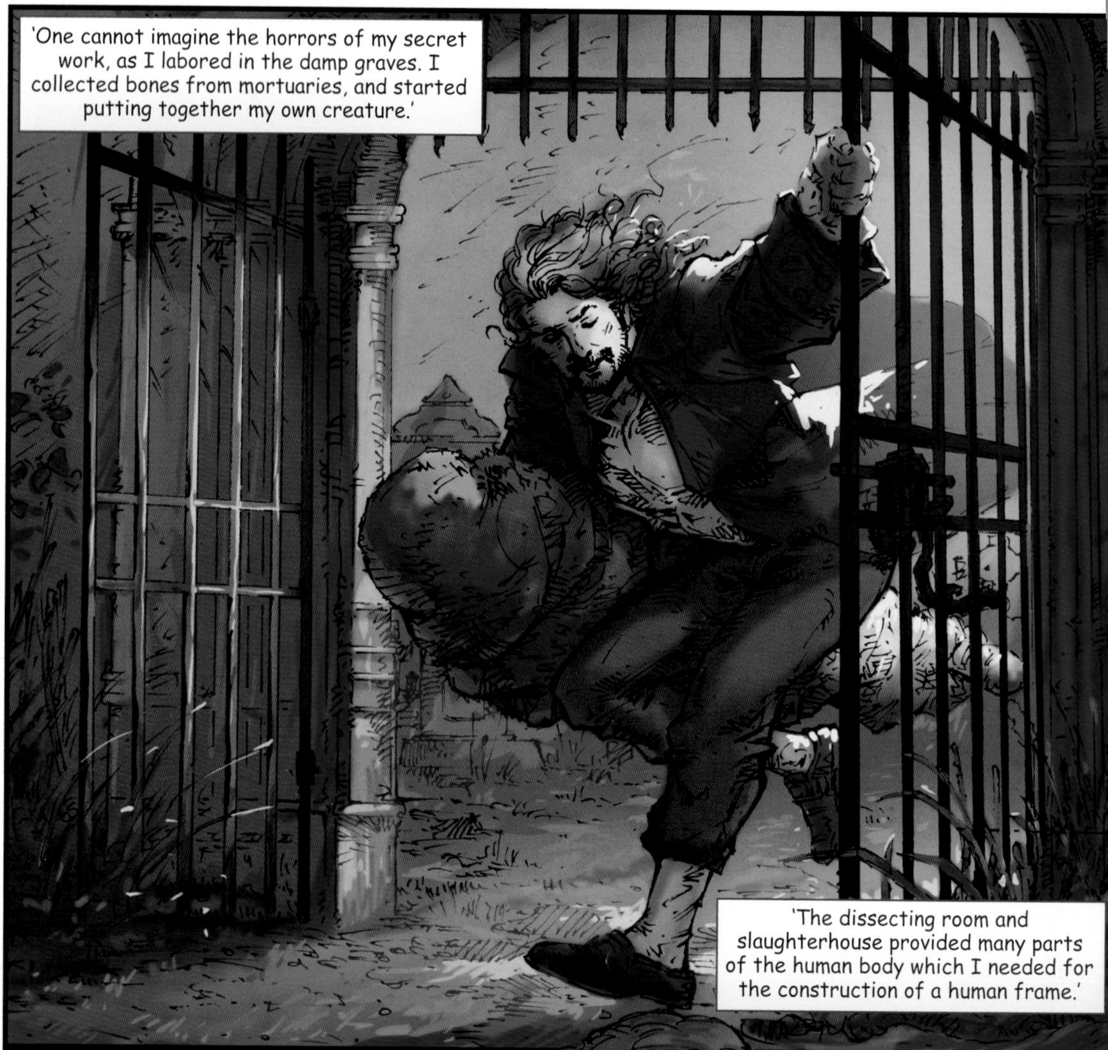
'One cannot imagine the horrors of my secret work, as I labored in the damp graves. I collected bones from mortuaries, and started putting together my own creature.'
'The dissecting room and slaughterhouse provided many parts of the human body which I needed for the construction of a human frame.'

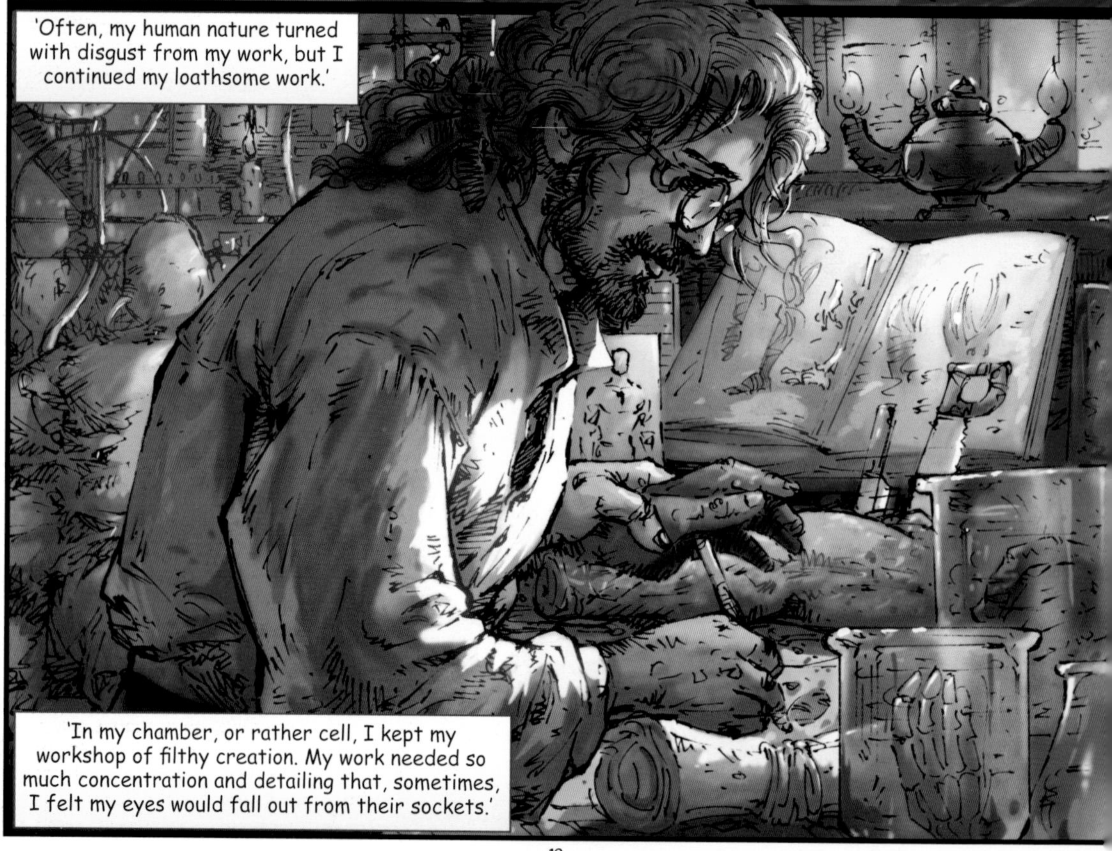
'Often, my human nature turned with disgust from my work, but I continued my loathsome work.'
'In my chamber, or rather cell, I kept my workshop of filthy creation. My work needed so much concentration and detailing that, sometimes, I felt my eyes would fall out from their sockets.'

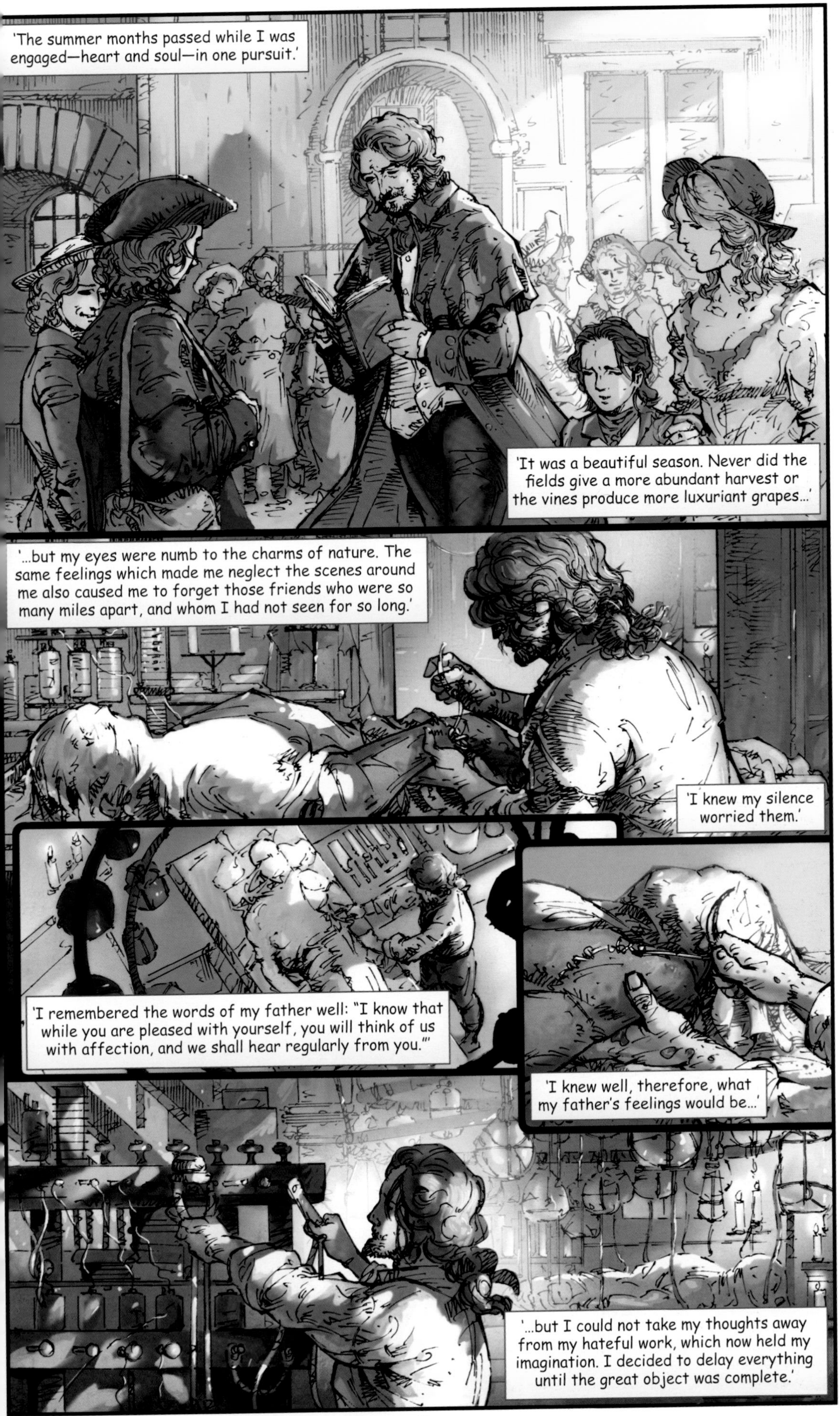
'The summer months passed while I was engaged—heart and soul—in one pursuit.'
'It was a beautiful season. Never did the fields give a more abundant harvest or the vines produce more luxuriant grapes...'
'...but my eyes were numb to the charms of nature. The same feelings which made me neglect the scenes around me also caused me to forget those friends who were so many miles apart, and whom I had not seen for so long.'
'I knew my silence worried them.'
'I remembered the words of my father well: "I know that while you are pleased with yourself, you will think of us with affection, and we shall hear regularly from you."'
'I knew well, therefore, what my father's feelings would be...'
'...but I could not take my thoughts away from my hateful work, which now held my imagination. I decided to delay everything until the great object was complete.'

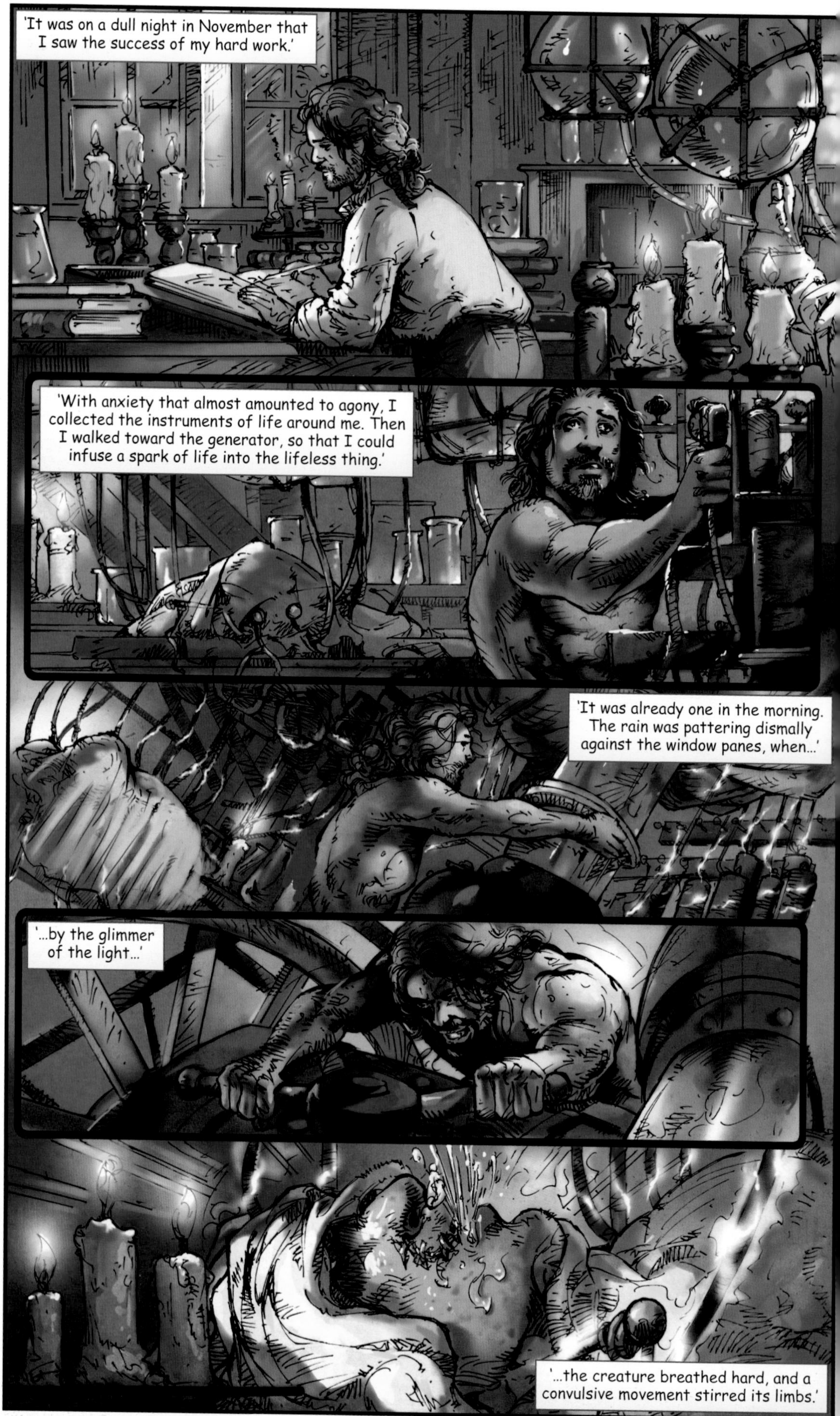
'It was on a dull night in November that I saw the success of my hard work.'
'With anxiety that almost amounted to agony, I collected the instruments of life around me. Then I walked toward the generator, so that I could infuse a spark of life into the lifeless thing.'
'It was already one in the morning. The rain was pattering dismally against the window panes, when...'
'...by the glimmer of the light...'
'...the creature breathed hard, and a convulsive movement stirred its limbs.'

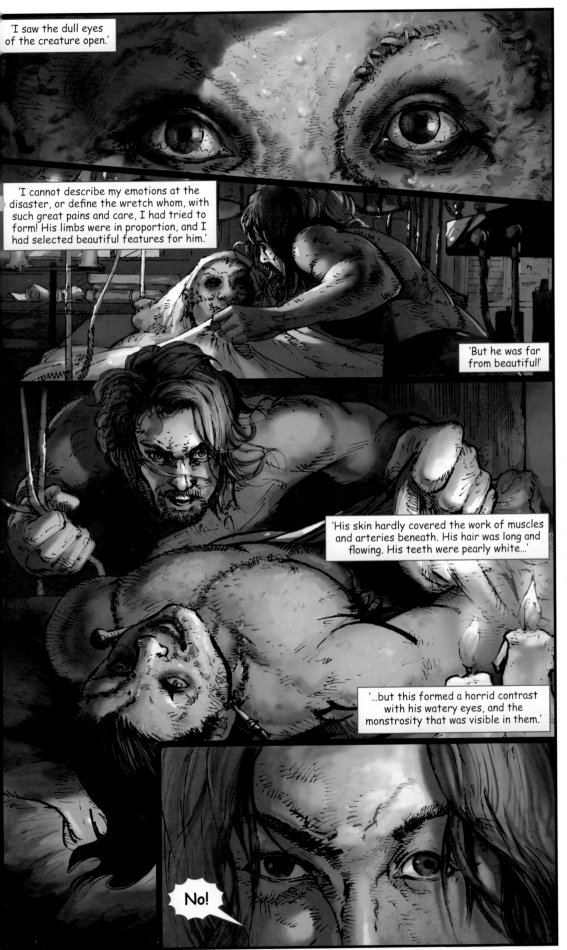

'I saw the dull eyes of the creature open.'

'I cannot describe my emotions at the disaster, or define the wretch whom, with such great pains and care, I had tried to form! His limbs were in proportion, and I had selected beautiful features for him.'

'But he was far from beautiful!'

'His skin hardly covered the work of muscles and arteries beneath. His hair was long and flowing. His teeth were pearly white...'

'...but this formed a horrid contrast with his watery eyes, and the monstrosity that was visible in them.'

No!

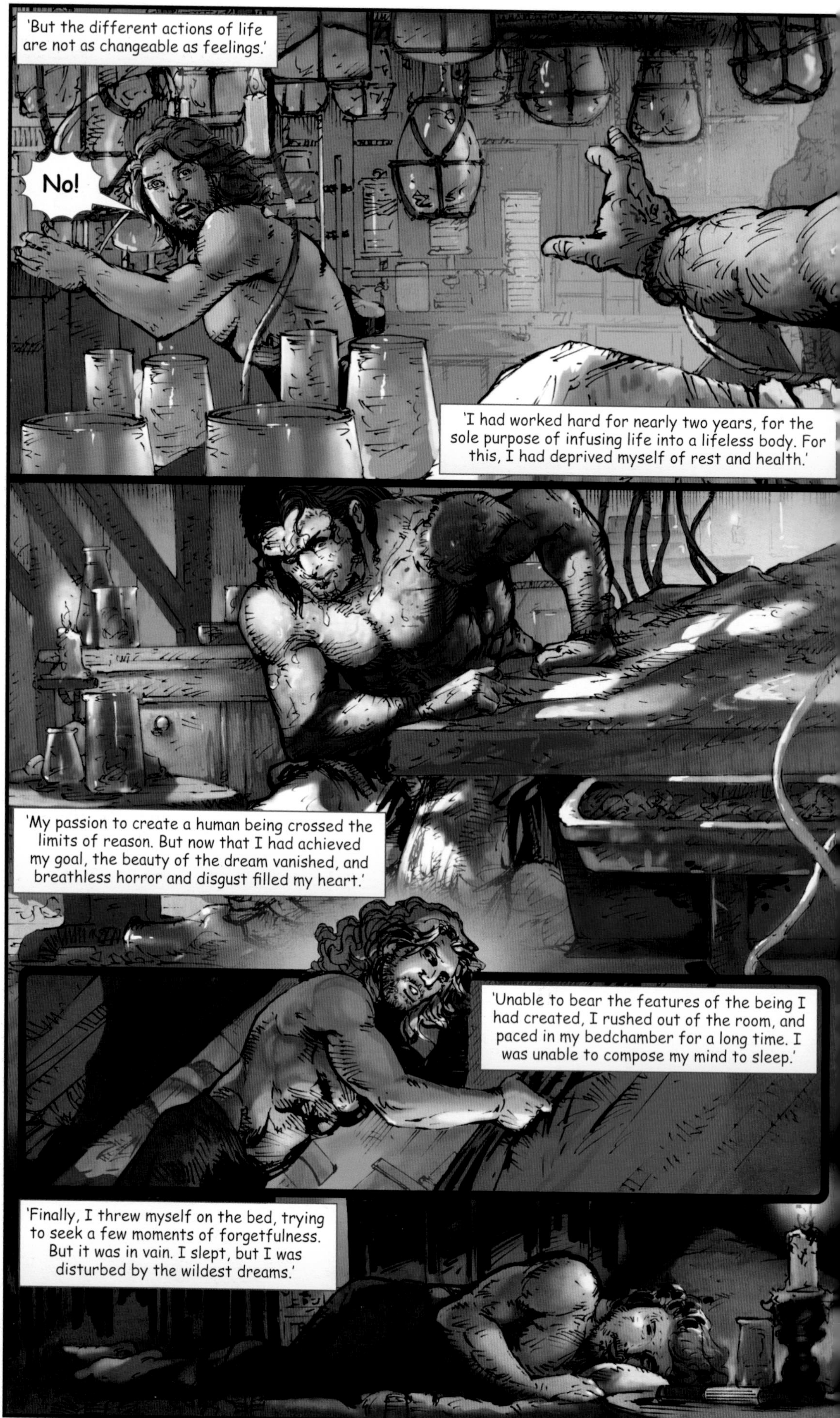
'But the different actions of life are not as changeable as feelings.'
No!
'I had worked hard for nearly two years, for the sole purpose of infusing life into a lifeless body. For this, I had deprived myself of rest and health.'
'My passion to create a human being crossed the limits of reason. But now that I had achieved my goal, the beauty of the dream vanished, and breathless horror and disgust filled my heart.'
'Unable to bear the features of the being I had created, I rushed out of the room, and paced in my bedchamber for a long time. I was unable to compose my mind to sleep.'
'Finally, I threw myself on the bed, trying to seek a few moments of forgetfulness. But it was in vain. I slept, but I was disturbed by the wildest dreams.'

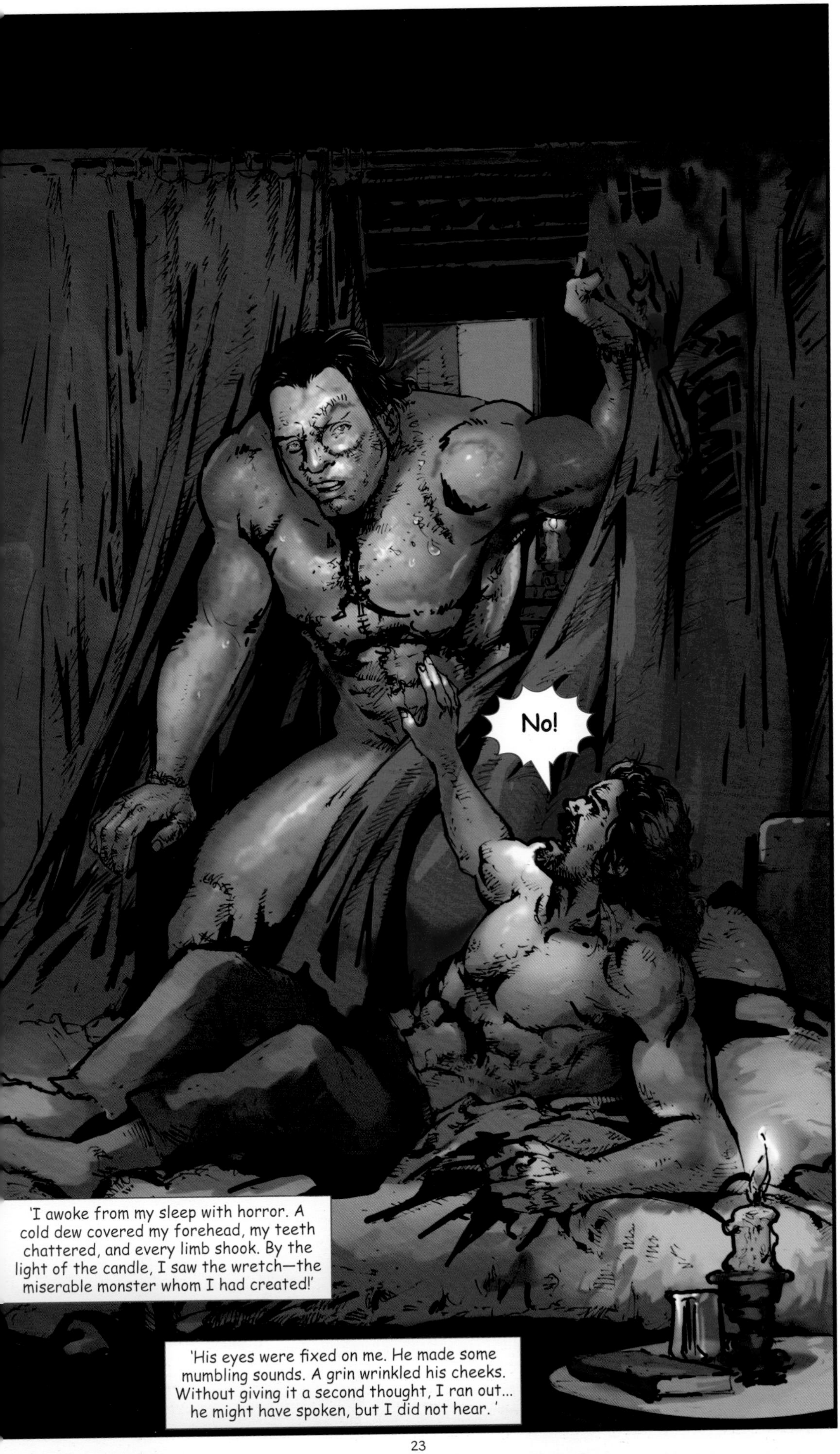
No!
'I awoke from my sleep with horror. A cold dew covered my forehead, my teeth chattered, and every limb shook. By the light of the candle, I saw the wretch—the miserable monster whom I had created!'
'His eyes were fixed on me. He made some mumbling sounds. A grin wrinkled his cheeks. Without giving it a second thought, I ran out... he might have spoken, but I did not hear.'

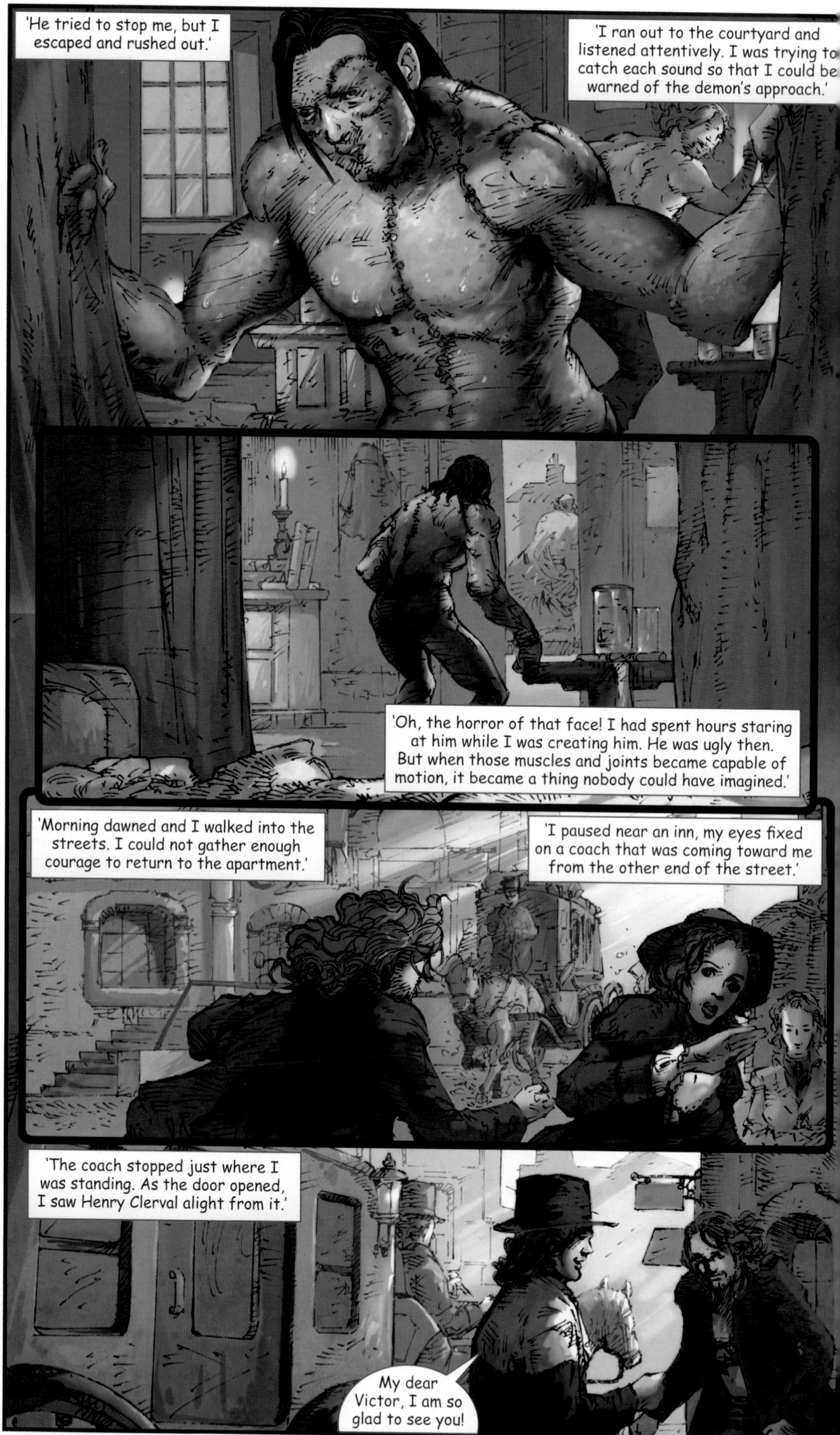
'He tried to stop me, but I escaped and rushed out.'
'I ran out to the courtyard and listened attentively. I was trying to catch each sound so that I could be warned of the demon's approach.'
'Oh, the horror of that face! I had spent hours staring at him while I was creating him. He was ugly then. But when those muscles and joints became capable of motion, it became a thing nobody could have imagined.'
'Morning dawned and I walked into the streets. I could not gather enough courage to return to the apartment.'
'I paused near an inn, my eyes fixed on a coach that was coming toward me from the other end of the street.'
'The coach stopped just where I was standing. As the door opened, I saw Henry Clerval alight from it.'
My dear Victor, I am so glad to see you!

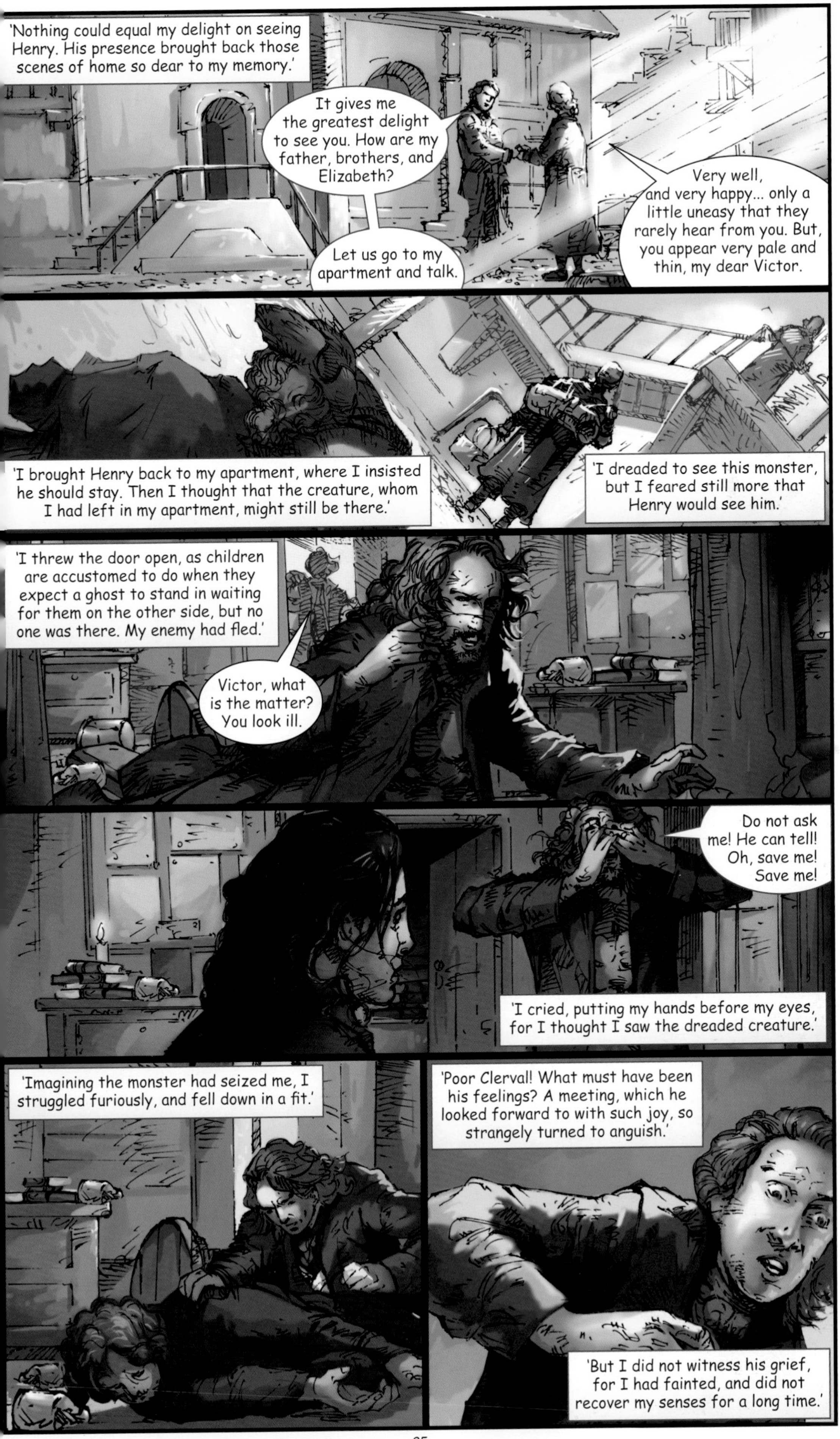

'Nothing could equal my delight on seeing Henry. His presence brought back those scenes of home so dear to my memory.'
It gives me the greatest delight to see you. How are my father, brothers, and Elizabeth?
Very well, and very happy... only a little uneasy that they rarely hear from you. But, you appear very pale and thin, my dear Victor.
Let us go to my apartment and talk.
'I brought Henry back to my apartment, where I insisted he should stay. Then I thought that the creature, whom I had left in my apartment, might still be there.'
'I dreaded to see this monster, but I feared still more that Henry would see him.'
'I threw the door open, as children are accustomed to do when they expect a ghost to stand in waiting for them on the other side, but no one was there. My enemy had fled.'
Victor, what is the matter? You look ill.
Do not ask me! He can tell! Oh, save me! Save me!
'I cried, putting my hands before my eyes, for I thought I saw the dreaded creature.'
'Imagining the monster had seized me, I struggled furiously, and fell down in a fit.'
'Poor Clerval! What must have been his feelings? A meeting, which he looked forward to with such joy, so strangely turned to anguish.'
'But I did not witness his grief, for I had fainted, and did not recover my senses for a long time.'

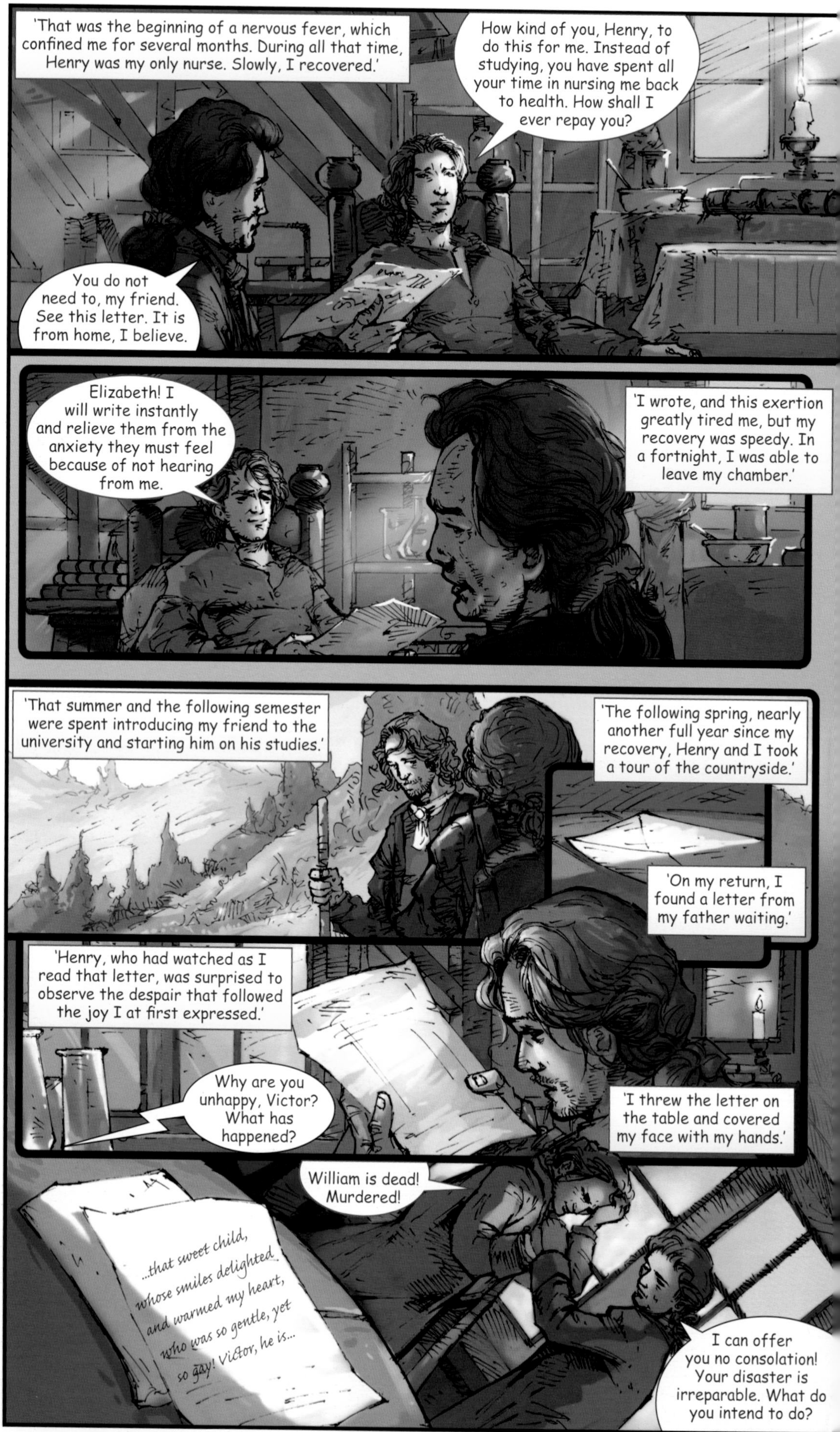
'That was the beginning of a nervous fever, which confined me for several months. During all that time, Henry was my only nurse. Slowly, I recovered.'
How kind of you, Henry, to do this for me. Instead of studying, you have spent all your time in nursing me back to health. How shall I ever repay you?
You do not need to, my friend. See this letter. It is from home, I believe.
Elizabeth! I will write instantly and relieve them from the anxiety they must feel because of not hearing from me.
'I wrote, and this exertion greatly tired me, but my recovery was speedy. In a fortnight, I was able to leave my chamber.'
'That summer and the following semester were spent introducing my friend to the university and starting him on his studies.'
'The following spring, nearly another full year since my recovery, Henry and I took a tour of the countryside.'
'On my return, I found a letter from my father waiting.'
'Henry, who had watched as I read that letter, was surprised to observe the despair that followed the joy I at first expressed.'
Why are you unhappy, Victor? What has happened?
'I threw the letter on the table and covered my face with my hands.'
William is dead! Murdered!
...that sweet child, whose smiles delighted and warmed my heart, who was so gentle, yet so gay! Victor, he is...
I can offer you no consolation! Your disaster is irreparable. What do you intend to do?

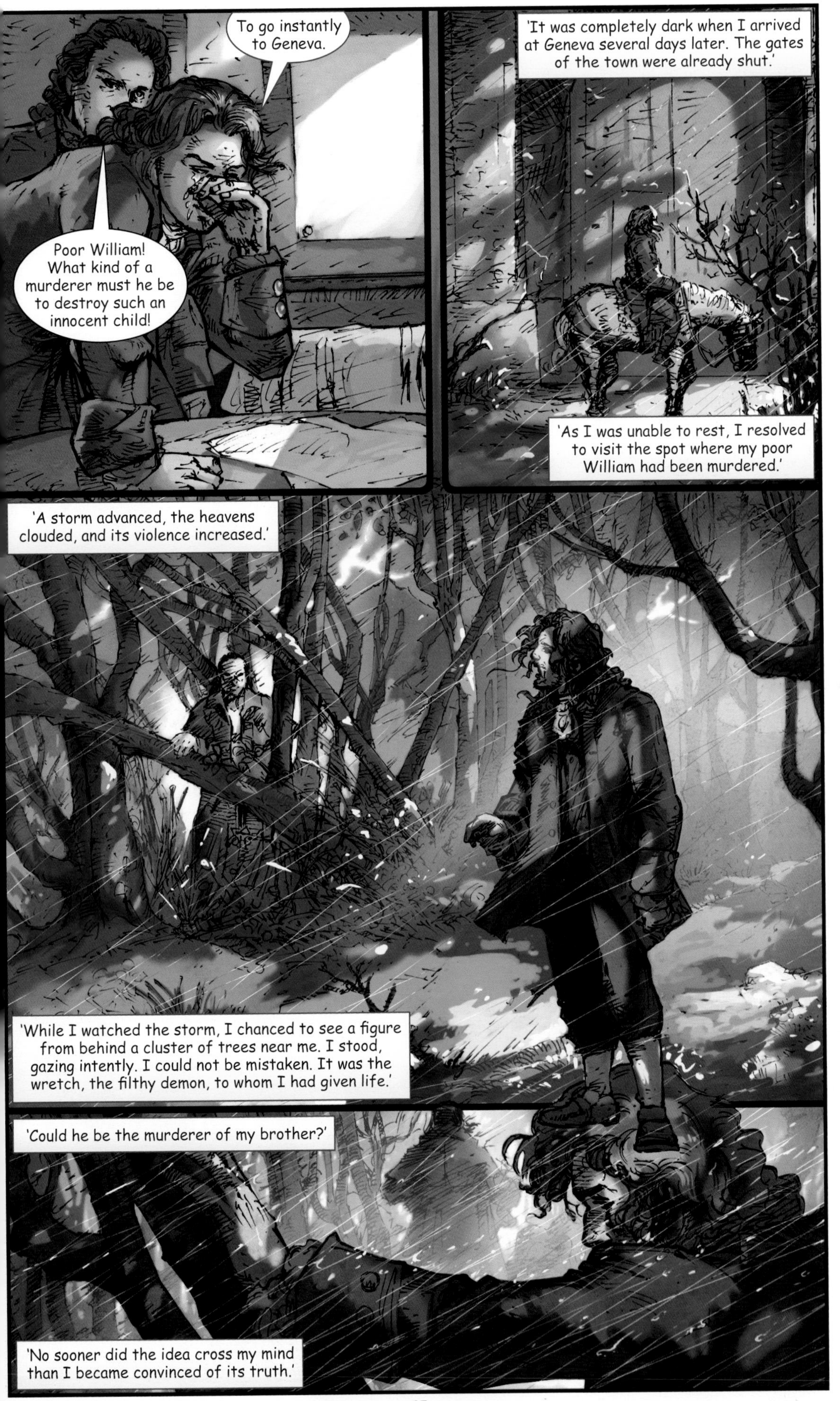
To go instantly to Geneva.
Poor William! What kind of a murderer must he be to destroy such an innocent child!
'It was completely dark when I arrived at Geneva several days later. The gates of the town were already shut.'
'As I was unable to rest, I resolved to visit the spot where my poor William had been murdered.'
'A storm advanced, the heavens clouded, and its violence increased.'
'While I watched the storm, I chanced to see a figure from behind a cluster of trees near me. I stood, gazing intently. I could not be mistaken. It was the wretch, the filthy demon, to whom I had given life.'
'Could he be the murderer of my brother?'
'No sooner did the idea cross my mind than I became convinced of its truth.'

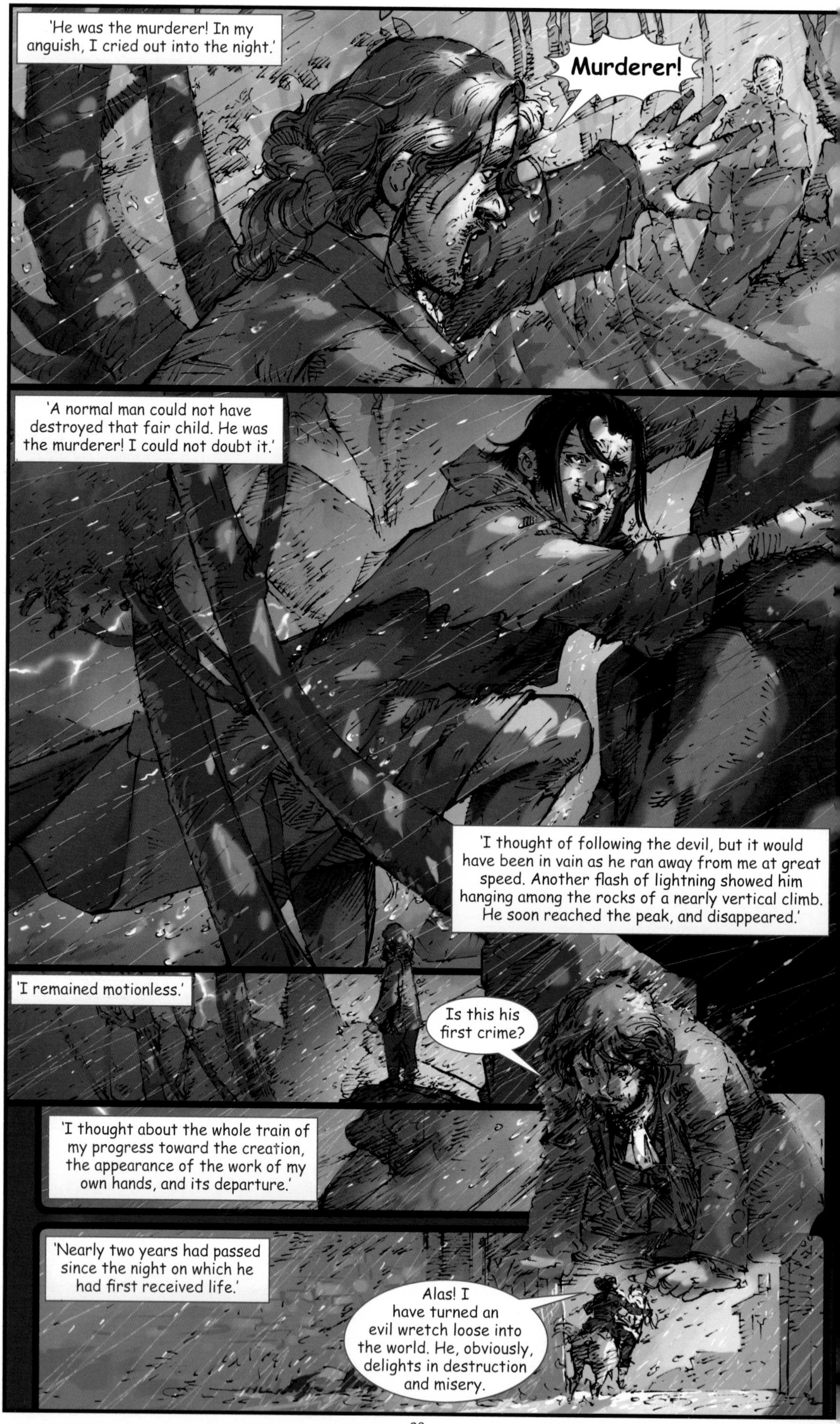
'He was the murderer! In my anguish, I cried out into the night.'
Murderer!
'A normal man could not have destroyed that fair child. He was the murderer! I could not doubt it.'
'I thought of following the devil, but it would have been in vain as he ran away from me at great speed. Another flash of lightning showed him hanging among the rocks of a nearly vertical climb. He soon reached the peak, and disappeared.'
'I remained motionless.'
Is this his first crime?
'I thought about the whole train of my progress toward the creation, the appearance of the work of my own hands, and its departure.'
'Nearly two years had passed since the night on which he had first received life.'
Alas! I have turned an evil wretch loose into the world. He, obviously, delights in destruction and misery.

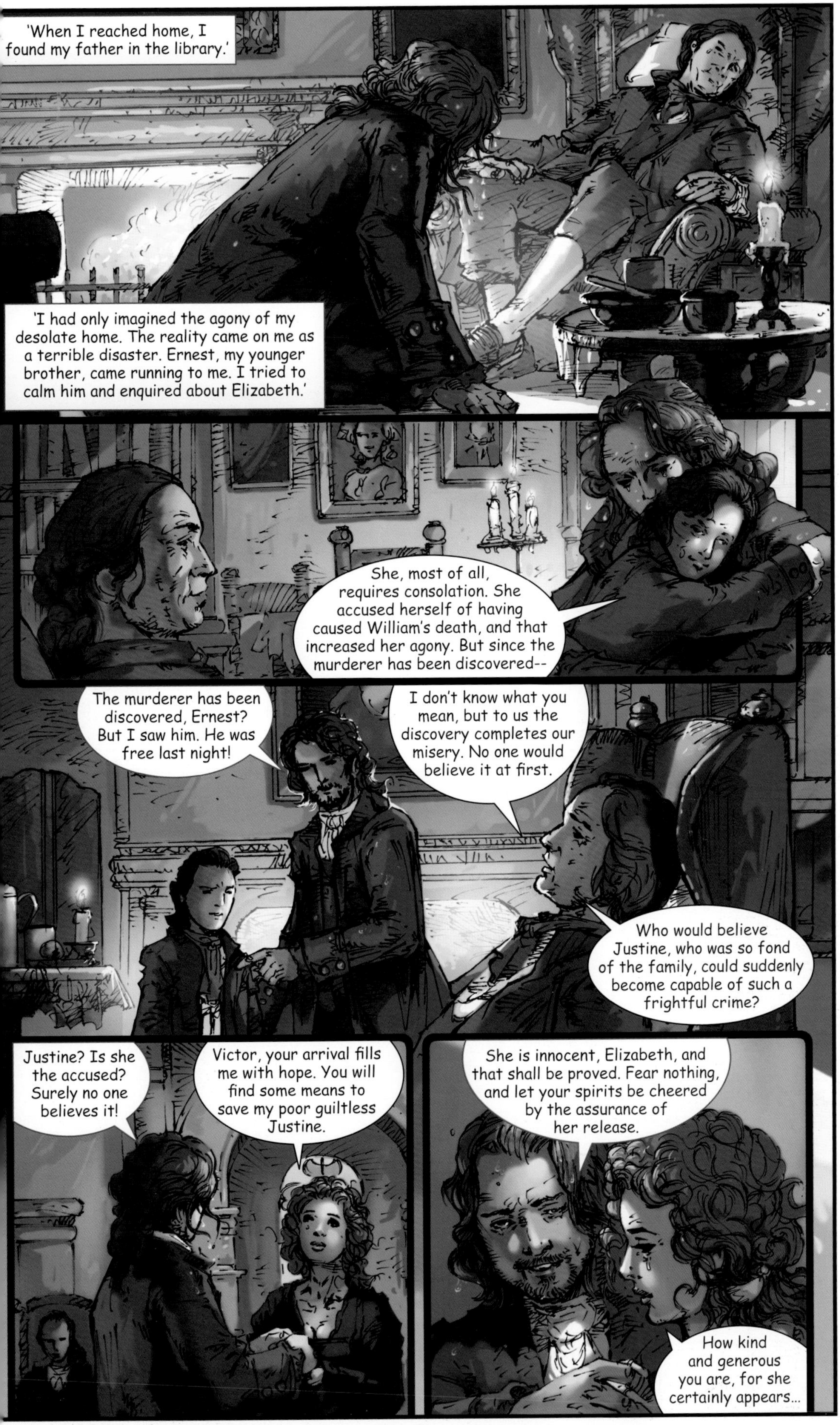
'When I reached home, I found my father in the library.'
'I had only imagined the agony of my desolate home. The reality came on me as a terrible disaster. Ernest, my younger brother, came running to me. I tried to calm him and enquired about Elizabeth.'
She, most of all, requires consolation. She accused herself of having caused William's death, and that increased her agony. But since the murderer has been discovered--
The murderer has been discovered, Ernest? But I saw him. He was free last night!
I don't know what you mean, but to us the discovery completes our misery. No one would believe it at first.
Who would believe Justine, who was so fond of the family, could suddenly become capable of such a frightful crime?
Justine? Is she the accused? Surely no one believes it!
Victor, your arrival fills me with hope. You will find some means to save my poor guiltless Justine.
She is innocent, Elizabeth, and that shall be proved. Fear nothing, and let your spirits be cheered by the assurance of her release.
How kind and generous you are, for she certainly appears...

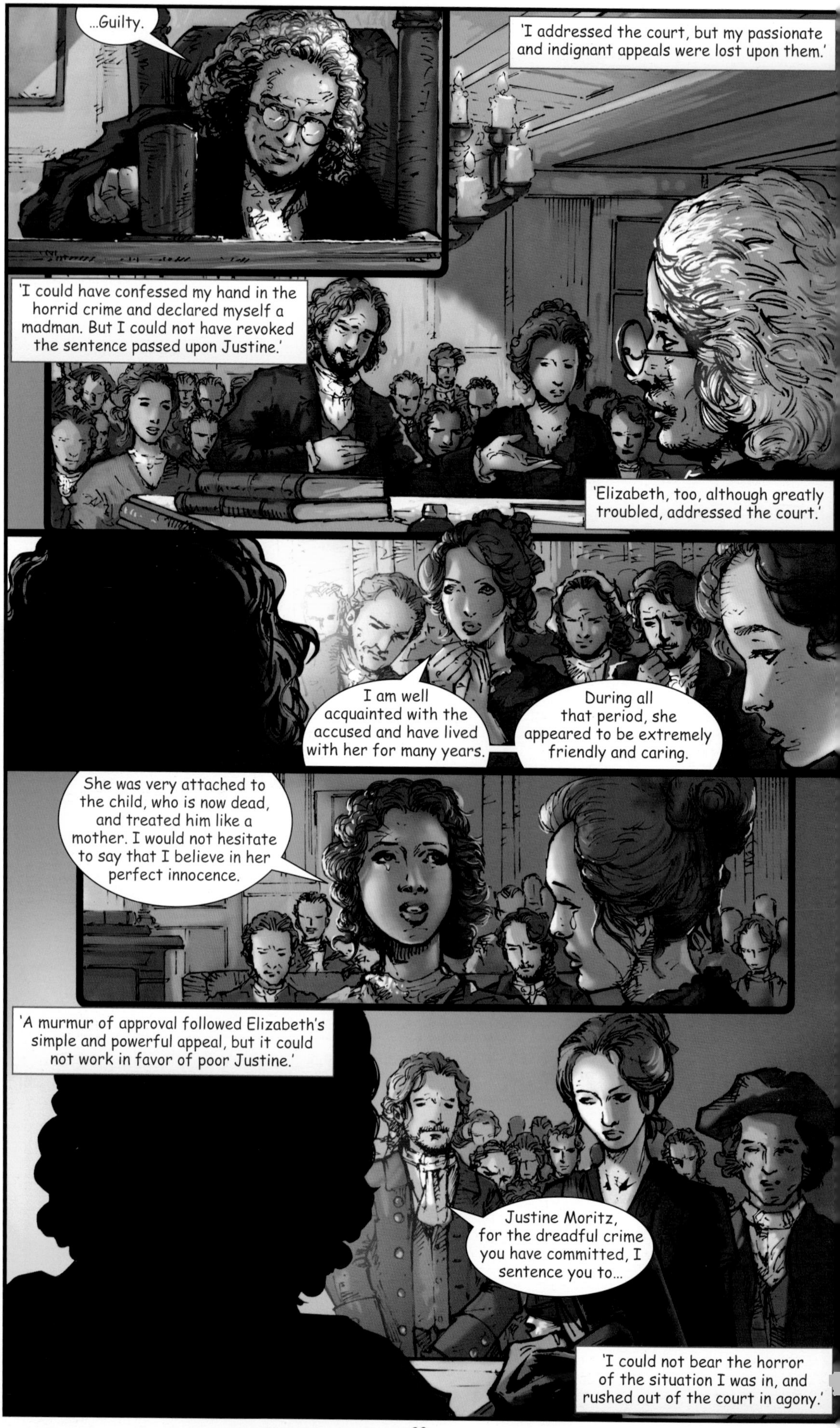
...Guilty.
'I addressed the court, but my passionate and indignant appeals were lost upon them.'
'I could have confessed my hand in the horrid crime and declared myself a madman. But I could not have revoked the sentence passed upon Justine.'
'Elizabeth, too, although greatly troubled, addressed the court.'
I am well acquainted with the accused and have lived with her for many years.
During all that period, she appeared to be extremely friendly and caring.
She was very attached to the child, who is now dead, and treated him like a mother. I would not hesitate to say that I believe in her perfect innocence.
'A murmur of approval followed Elizabeth's simple and powerful appeal, but it could not work in favor of poor Justine.'
Justine Moritz, for the dreadful crime you have committed, I sentence you to...
'I could not bear the horror of the situation I was in, and rushed out of the court in agony.'

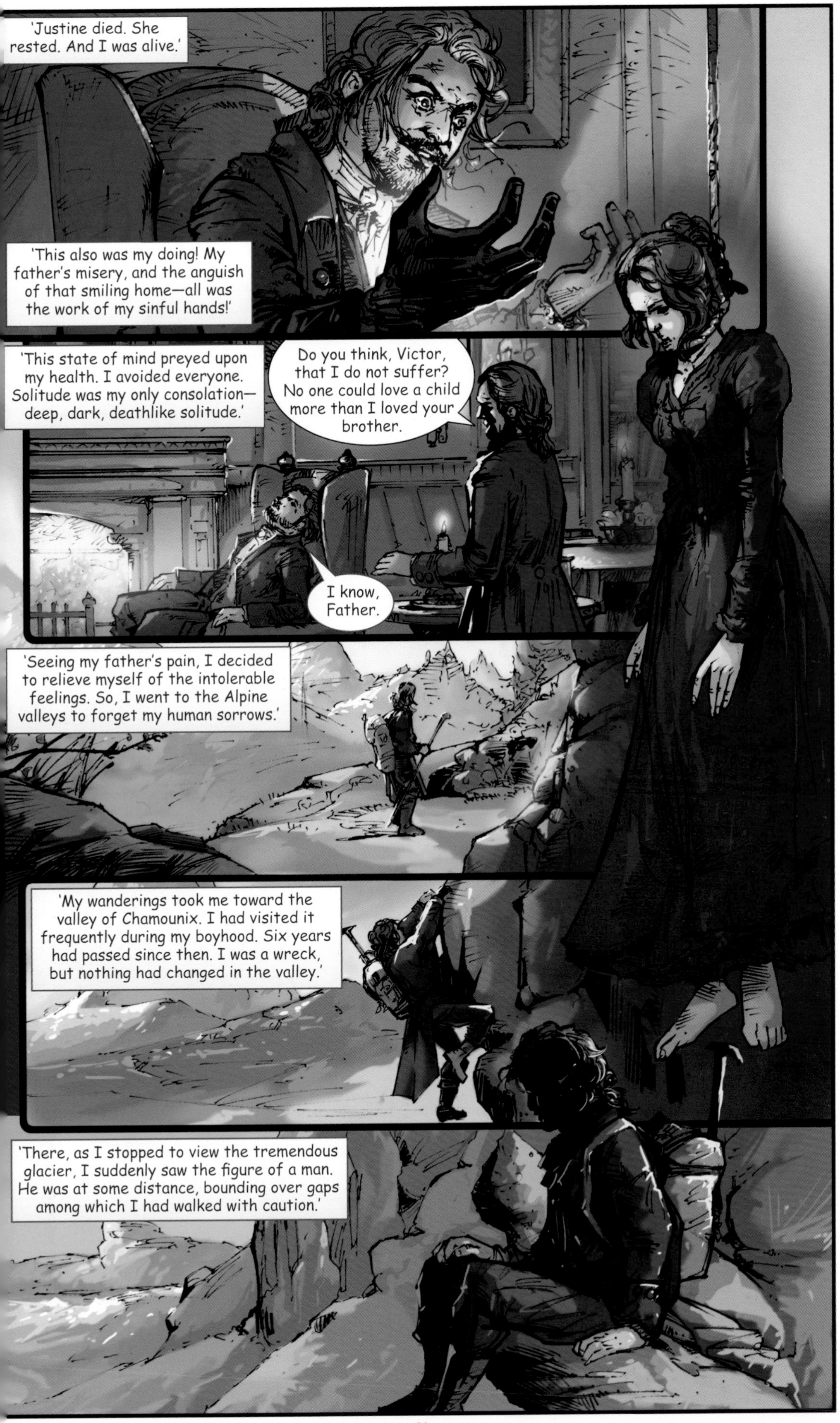
'Justine died. She rested. And I was alive.'
'This also was my doing! My father's misery, and the anguish of that smiling home—all was the work of my sinful hands!'
'This state of mind preyed upon my health. I avoided everyone. Solitude was my only consolation—deep, dark, deathlike solitude.'
Do you think, Victor, that I do not suffer? No one could love a child more than I loved your brother.
I know, Father.
'Seeing my father's pain, I decided to relieve myself of the intolerable feelings. So, I went to the Alpine valleys to forget my human sorrows.'
'My wanderings took me toward the valley of Chamounix. I had visited it frequently during my boyhood. Six years had passed since then. I was a wreck, but nothing had changed in the valley.'
'There, as I stopped to view the tremendous glacier, I suddenly saw the figure of a man. He was at some distance, bounding over gaps among which I had walked with caution.'

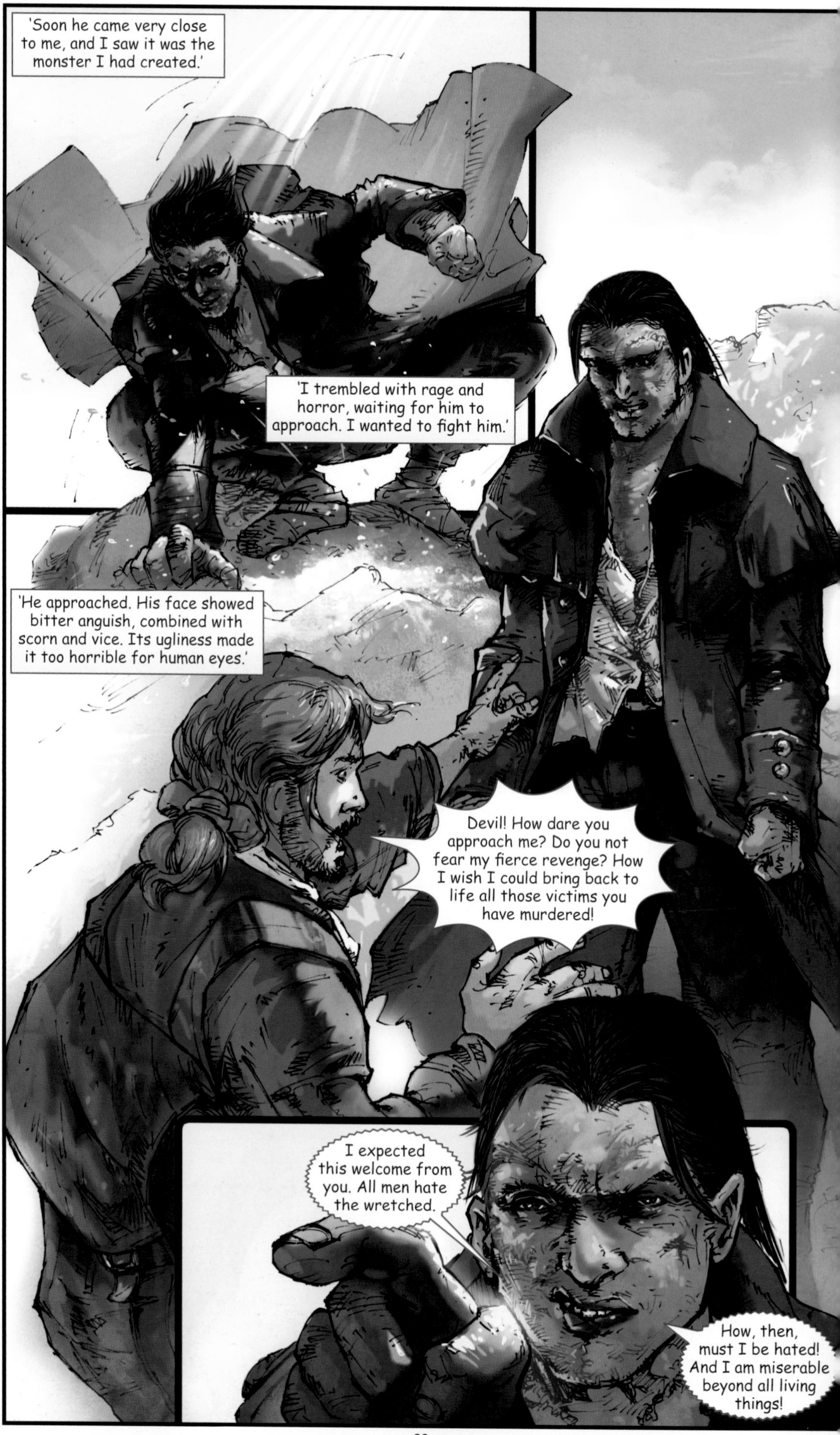
'Soon he came very close to me, and I saw it was the monster I had created.'
'I trembled with rage and horror, waiting for him to approach. I wanted to fight him.'
'He approached. His face showed bitter anguish, combined with scorn and vice. Its ugliness made it too horrible for human eyes.'
Devil! How dare you approach me? Do you not fear my fierce revenge? How I wish I could bring back to life all those victims you have murdered!
I expected this welcome from you. All men hate the wretched.
How, then, must I be hated! And I am miserable beyond all living things!

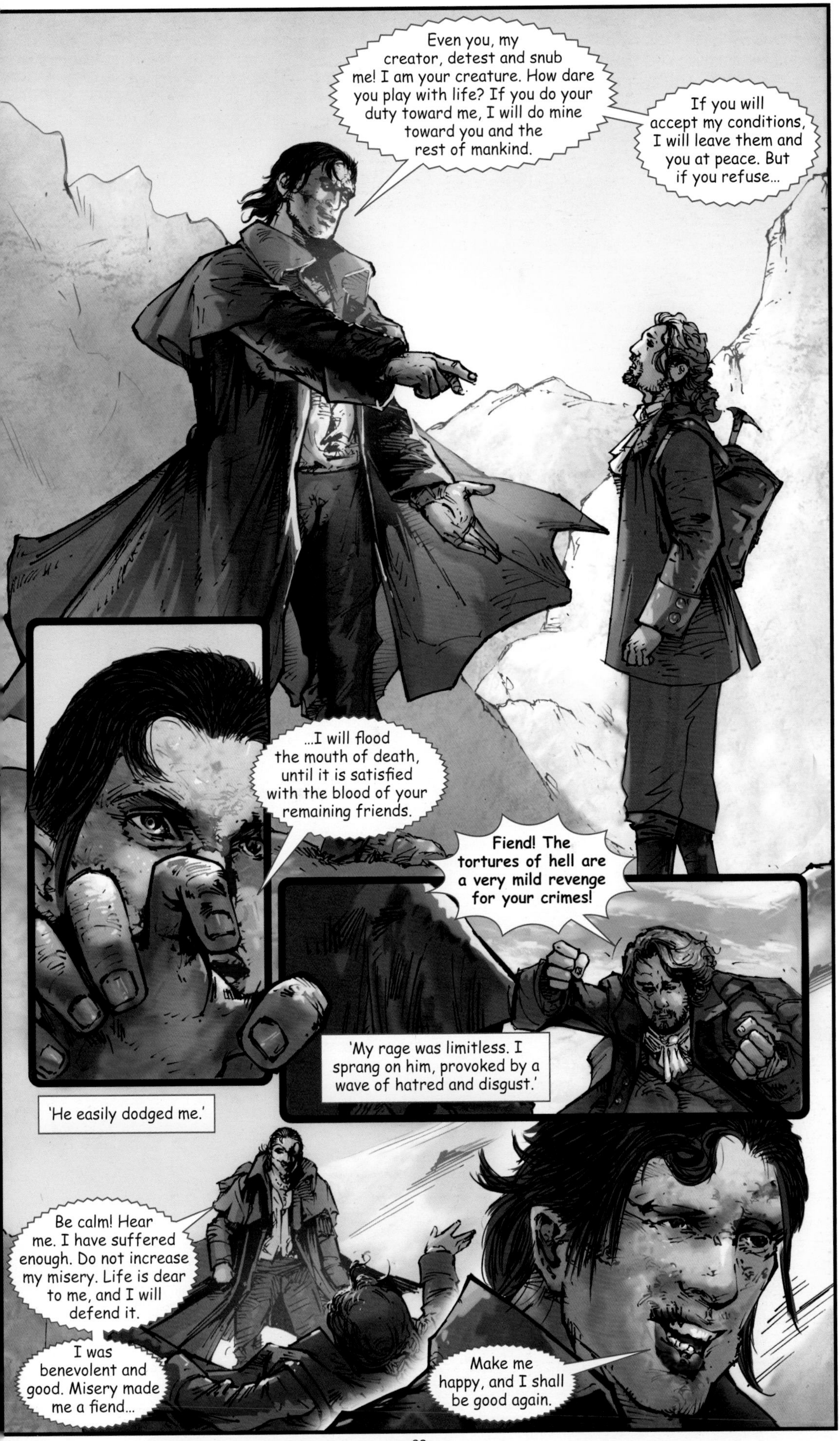
Even you, my creator, detest and snub me! I am your creature. How dare you play with life? If you do your duty toward me, I will do mine toward you and the rest of mankind.
If you will accept my conditions, I will leave them and you at peace. But if you refuse...
...I will flood the mouth of death, until it is satisfied with the blood of your remaining friends.
Fiend! The tortures of hell are a very mild revenge for your crimes!
'My rage was limitless. I sprang on him, provoked by a wave of hatred and disgust.'
'He easily dodged me.'
Be calm! Hear me. I have suffered enough. Do not increase my misery. Life is dear to me, and I will defend it.
I was benevolent and good. Misery made me a fiend...
Make me happy, and I shall be good again.

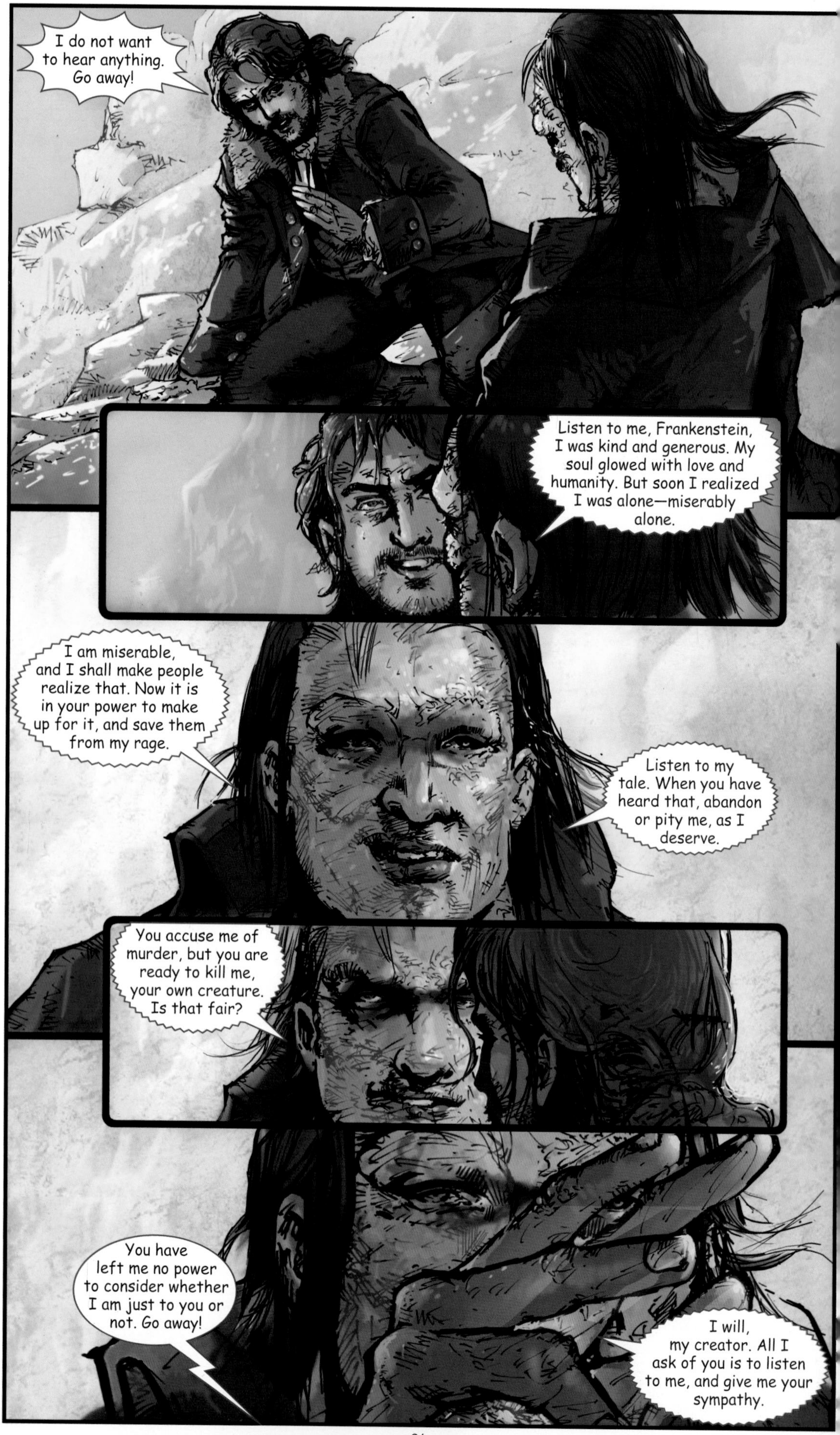
I do not want to hear anything. Go away!
Listen to me, Frankenstein, I was kind and generous. My soul glowed with love and humanity. But soon I realized I was alone—miserably alone.
I am miserable, and I shall make people realize that. Now it is in your power to make up for it, and save them from my rage.
Listen to my tale. When you have heard that, abandon or pity me, as I deserve.
You accuse me of murder, but you are ready to kill me, your own creature. Is that fair?
You have left me no power to consider whether I am just to you or not. Go away!
I will, my creator. All I ask of you is to listen to me, and give me your sympathy.

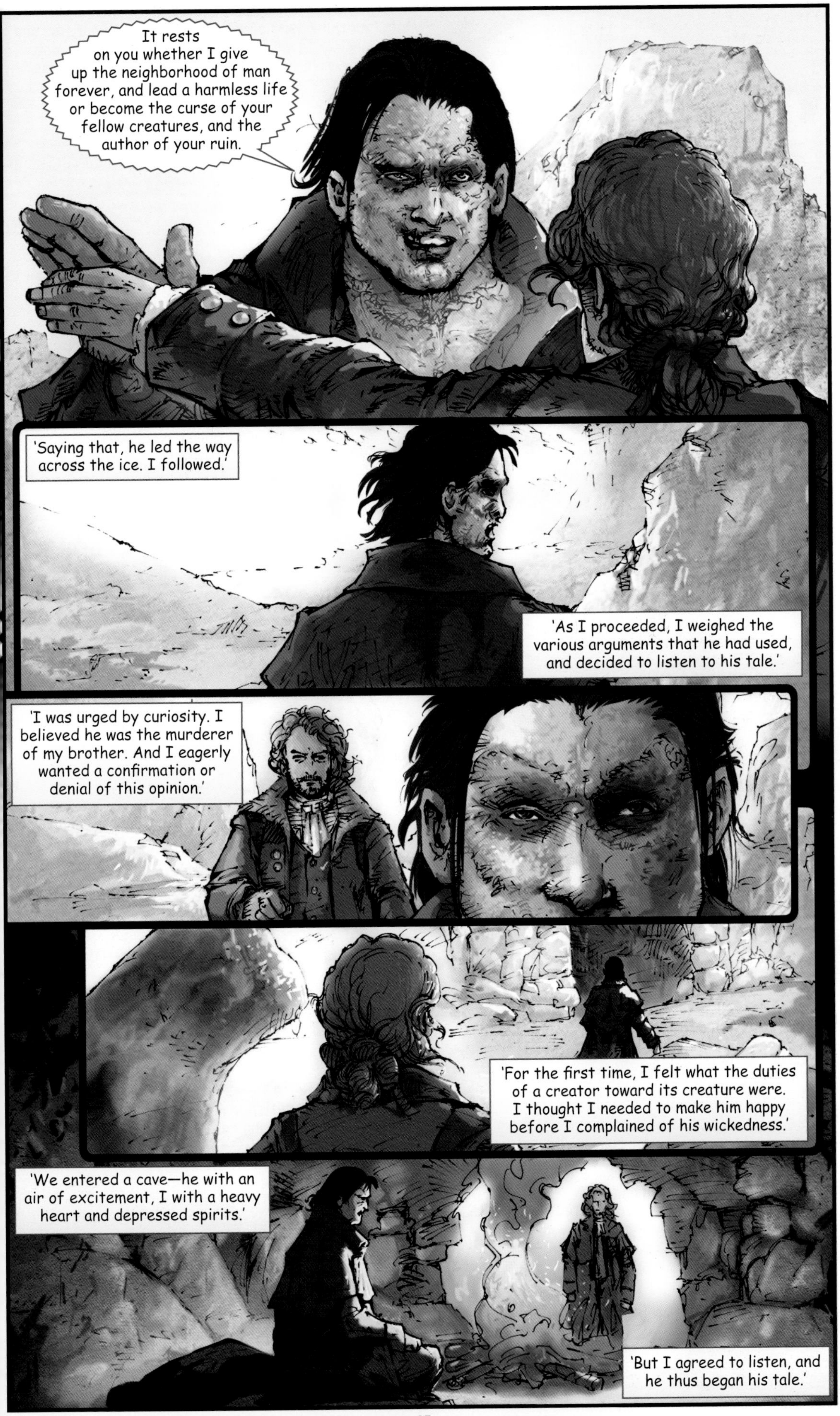
It rests on you whether I give up the neighborhood of man forever, and lead a harmless life or become the curse of your fellow creatures, and the author of your ruin.
'Saying that, he led the way across the ice. I followed.'
'As I proceeded, I weighed the various arguments that he had used, and decided to listen to his tale.'
'I was urged by curiosity. I believed he was the murderer of my brother. And I eagerly wanted a confirmation or denial of this opinion.'
'For the first time, I felt what the duties of a creator toward its creature were. I thought I needed to make him happy before I complained of his wickedness.'
'We entered a cave—he with an air of excitement, I with a heavy heart and depressed spirits.'
'But I agreed to listen, and he thus began his tale.'

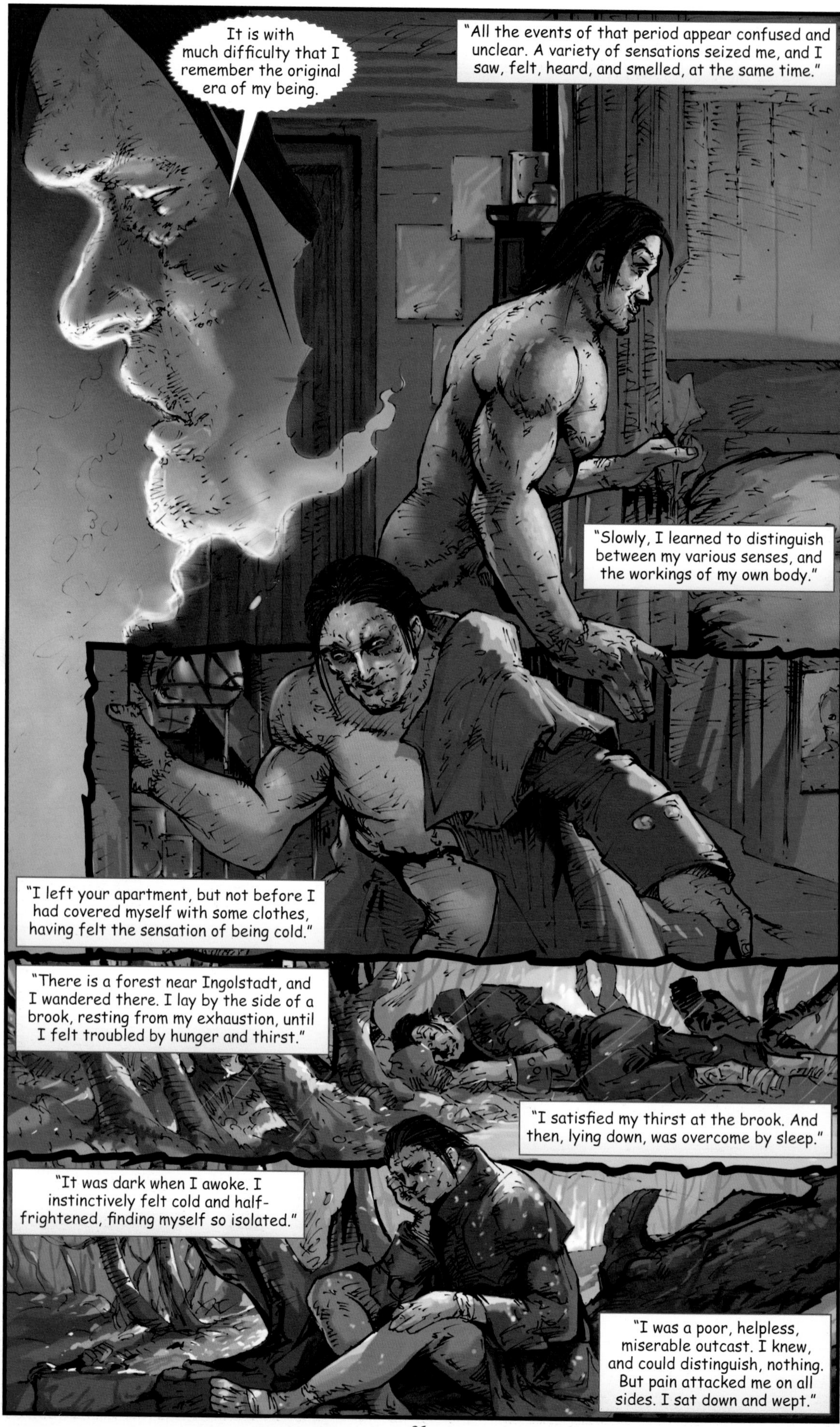
It is with much difficulty that I remember the original era of my being.
"All the events of that period appear confused and unclear. A variety of sensations seized me, and I saw, felt, heard, and smelled, at the same time."
"Slowly, I learned to distinguish between my various senses, and the workings of my own body."
"I left your apartment, but not before I had covered myself with some clothes, having felt the sensation of being cold."
"There is a forest near Ingolstadt, and I wandered there. I lay by the side of a brook, resting from my exhaustion, until I felt troubled by hunger and thirst."
"I satisfied my thirst at the brook. And then, lying down, was overcome by sleep."
"It was dark when I awoke. I instinctively felt cold and half-frightened, finding myself so isolated."
"I was a poor, helpless, miserable outcast. I knew, and could distinguish, nothing. But pain attacked me on all sides. I sat down and wept."

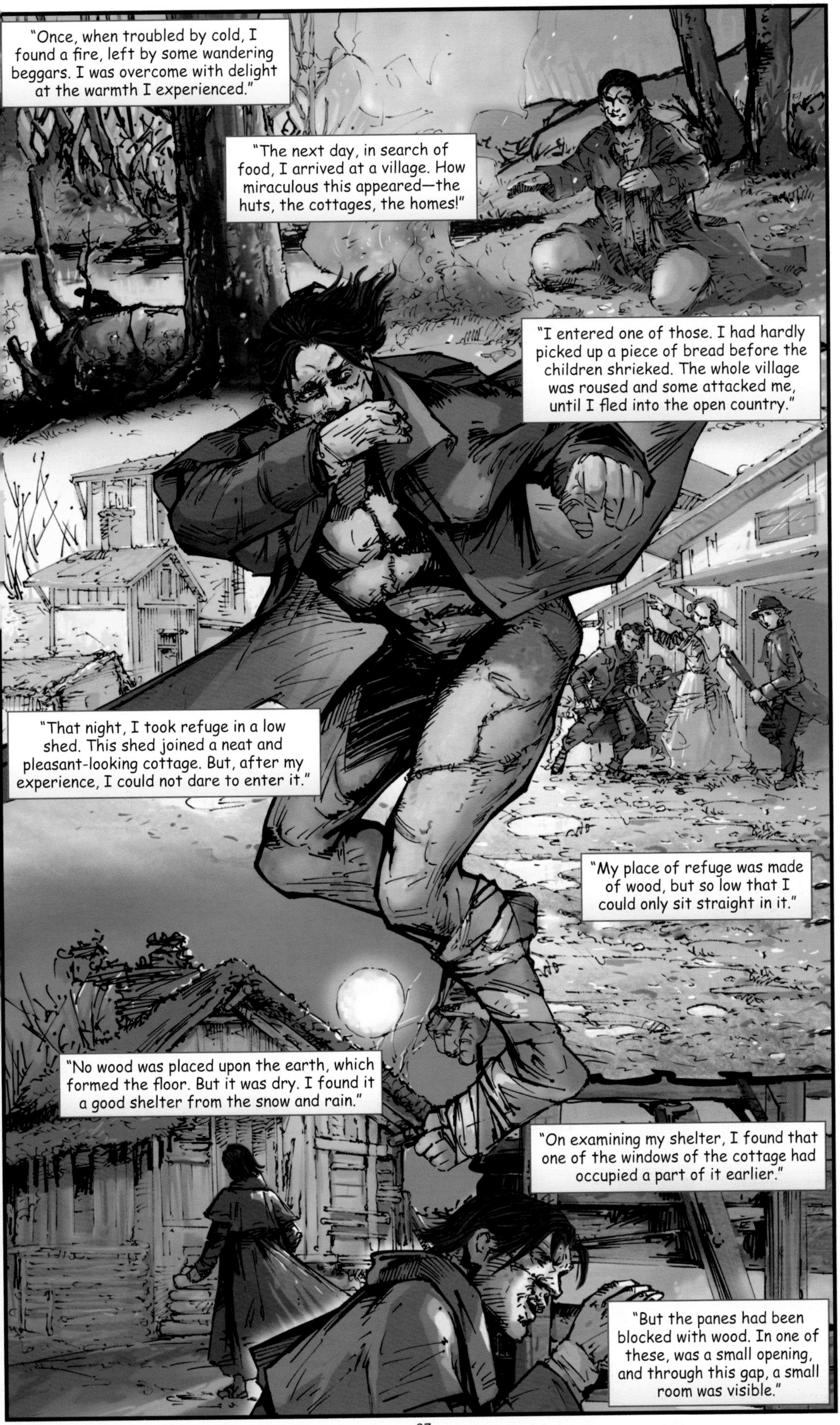
"Once, when troubled by cold, I found a fire, left by some wandering beggars. I was overcome with delight at the warmth I experienced."
"The next day, in search of food, I arrived at a village. How miraculous this appeared—the huts, the cottages, the homes!"
"I entered one of those. I had hardly picked up a piece of bread before the children shrieked. The whole village was roused and some attacked me, until I fled into the open country."
"That night, I took refuge in a low shed. This shed joined a neat and pleasant-looking cottage. But, after my experience, I could not dare to enter it."
"My place of refuge was made of wood, but so low that I could only sit straight in it."
"No wood was placed upon the earth, which formed the floor. But it was dry. I found it a good shelter from the snow and rain."
"On examining my shelter, I found that one of the windows of the cottage had occupied a part of it earlier."
"But the panes had been blocked with wood. In one of these, was a small opening, and through this gap, a small room was visible."

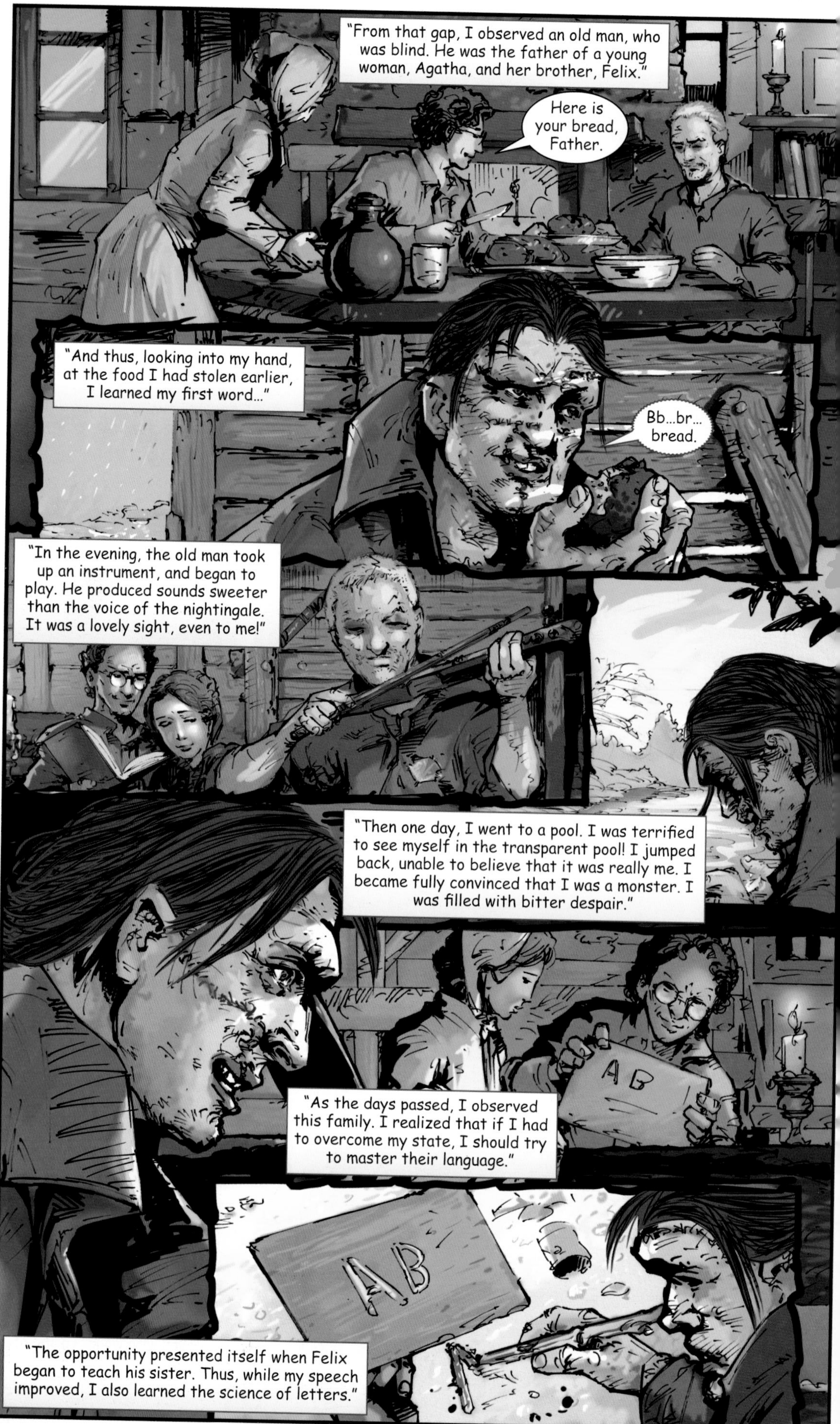
"From that gap, I observed an old man, who was blind. He was the father of a young woman, Agatha, and her brother, Felix."
Here is your bread, Father.
"And thus, looking into my hand, at the food I had stolen earlier, I learned my first word..."
Bb...br... bread.
"In the evening, the old man took up an instrument, and began to play. He produced sounds sweeter than the voice of the nightingale. It was a lovely sight, even to me!"
"Then one day, I went to a pool. I was terrified to see myself in the transparent pool! I jumped back, unable to believe that it was really me. I became fully convinced that I was a monster. I was filled with bitter despair."
AB
"As the days passed, I observed this family. I realized that if I had to overcome my state, I should try to master their language."
AB
"The opportunity presented itself when Felix began to teach his sister. Thus, while my speech improved, I also learned the science of letters."

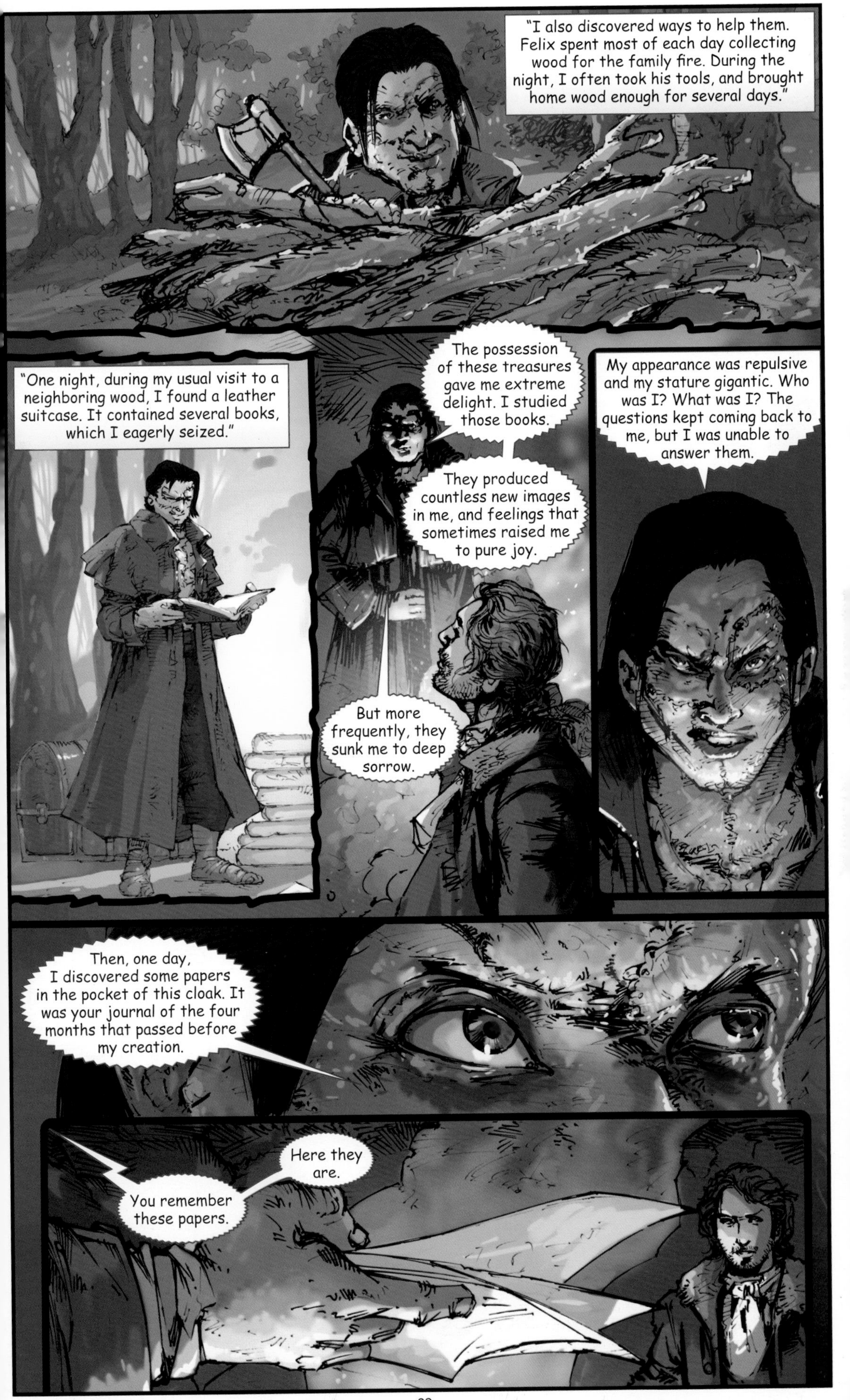
"I also discovered ways to help them. Felix spent most of each day collecting wood for the family fire. During the night, I often took his tools, and brought home wood enough for several days."
"One night, during my usual visit to a neighboring wood, I found a leather suitcase. It contained several books, which I eagerly seized."
The possession of these treasures gave me extreme delight. I studied those books.
They produced countless new images in me, and feelings that sometimes raised me to pure joy.
But more frequently, they sunk me to deep sorrow.
My appearance was repulsive and my stature gigantic. Who was I? What was I? The questions kept coming back to me, but I was unable to answer them.
Then, one day, I discovered some papers in the pocket of this cloak. It was your journal of the four months that passed before my creation.
Here they are.
You remember these papers.

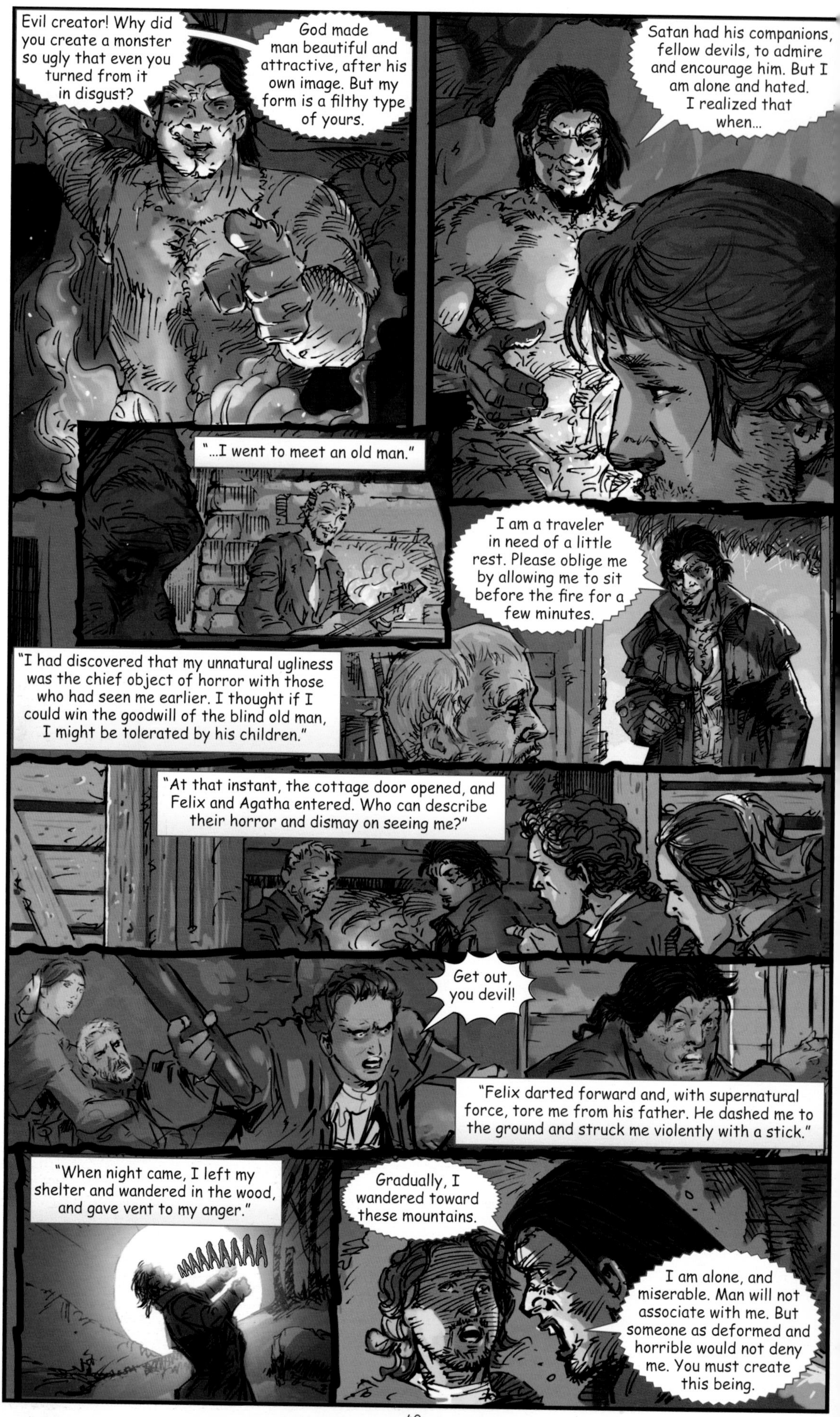
Evil creator! Why did you create a monster so ugly that even you turned from it in disgust?
God made man beautiful and attractive, after his own image. But my form is a filthy type of yours.
Satan had his companions, fellow devils, to admire and encourage him. But I am alone and hated. I realized that when...
"...I went to meet an old man."
"I had discovered that my unnatural ugliness was the chief object of horror with those who had seen me earlier. I thought if I could win the goodwill of the blind old man, I might be tolerated by his children."
I am a traveler in need of a little rest. Please oblige me by allowing me to sit before the fire for a few minutes.
"At that instant, the cottage door opened, and Felix and Agatha entered. Who can describe their horror and dismay on seeing me?"
Get out, you devil!
"Felix darted forward and, with supernatural force, tore me from his father. He dashed me to the ground and struck me violently with a stick."
"When night came, I left my shelter and wandered in the wood, and gave vent to my anger."
AAAAAAAA
Gradually, I wandered toward these mountains.
I am alone, and miserable. Man will not associate with me. But someone as deformed and horrible would not deny me. You must create this being.

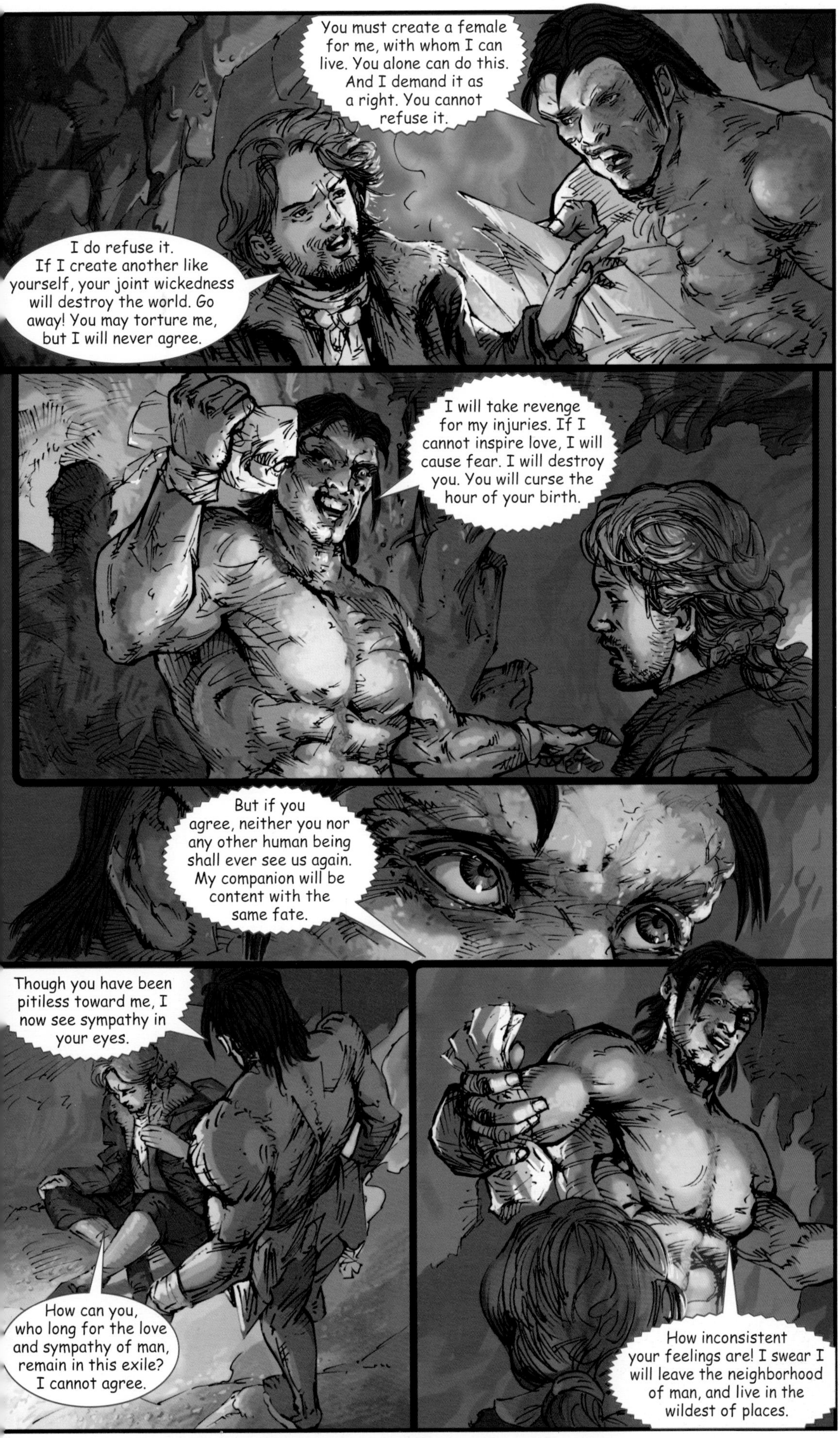
You must create a female for me, with whom I can live. You alone can do this. And I demand it as a right. You cannot refuse it.
I do refuse it. If I create another like yourself, your joint wickedness will destroy the world. Go away! You may torture me, but I will never agree.
I will take revenge for my injuries. If I cannot inspire love, I will cause fear. I will destroy you. You will curse the hour of your birth.
But if you agree, neither you nor any other human being shall ever see us again. My companion will be content with the same fate.
Though you have been pitiless toward me, I now see sympathy in your eyes.
How can you, who long for the love and sympathy of man, remain in this exile? I cannot agree.
How inconsistent your feelings are! I swear I will leave the neighborhood of man, and live in the wildest of places.

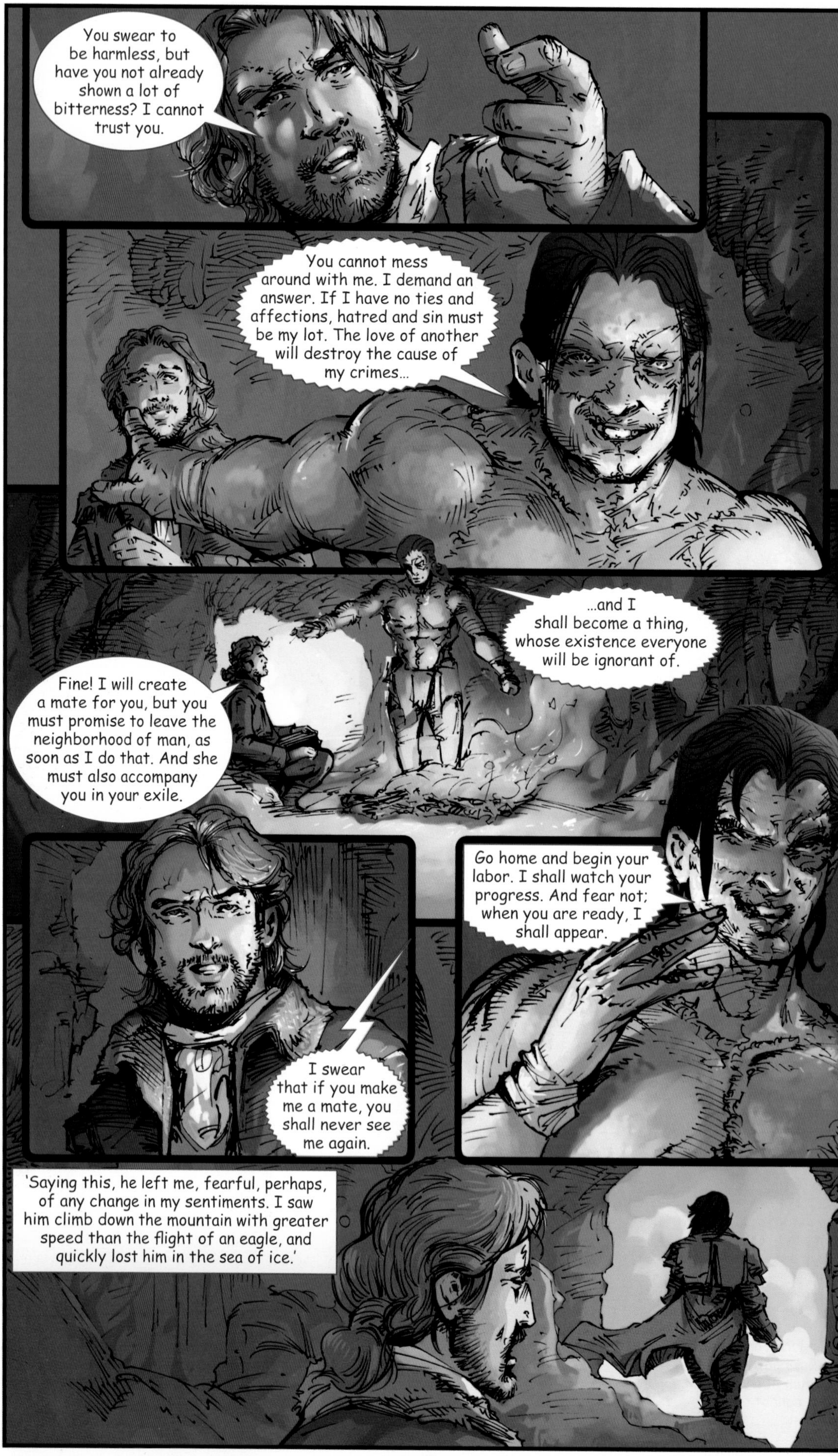
You swear to be harmless, but have you not already shown a lot of bitterness? I cannot trust you.
You cannot mess around with me. I demand an answer. If I have no ties and affections, hatred and sin must be my lot. The love of another will destroy the cause of my crimes...
...and I shall become a thing, whose existence everyone will be ignorant of.
Fine! I will create a mate for you, but you must promise to leave the neighborhood of man, as soon as I do that. And she must also accompany you in your exile.
I swear that if you make me a mate, you shall never see me again.
Go home and begin your labor. I shall watch your progress. And fear not; when you are ready, I shall appear.
'Saying this, he left me, fearful, perhaps, of any change in my sentiments. I saw him climb down the mountain with greater speed than the flight of an eagle, and quickly lost him in the sea of ice.'

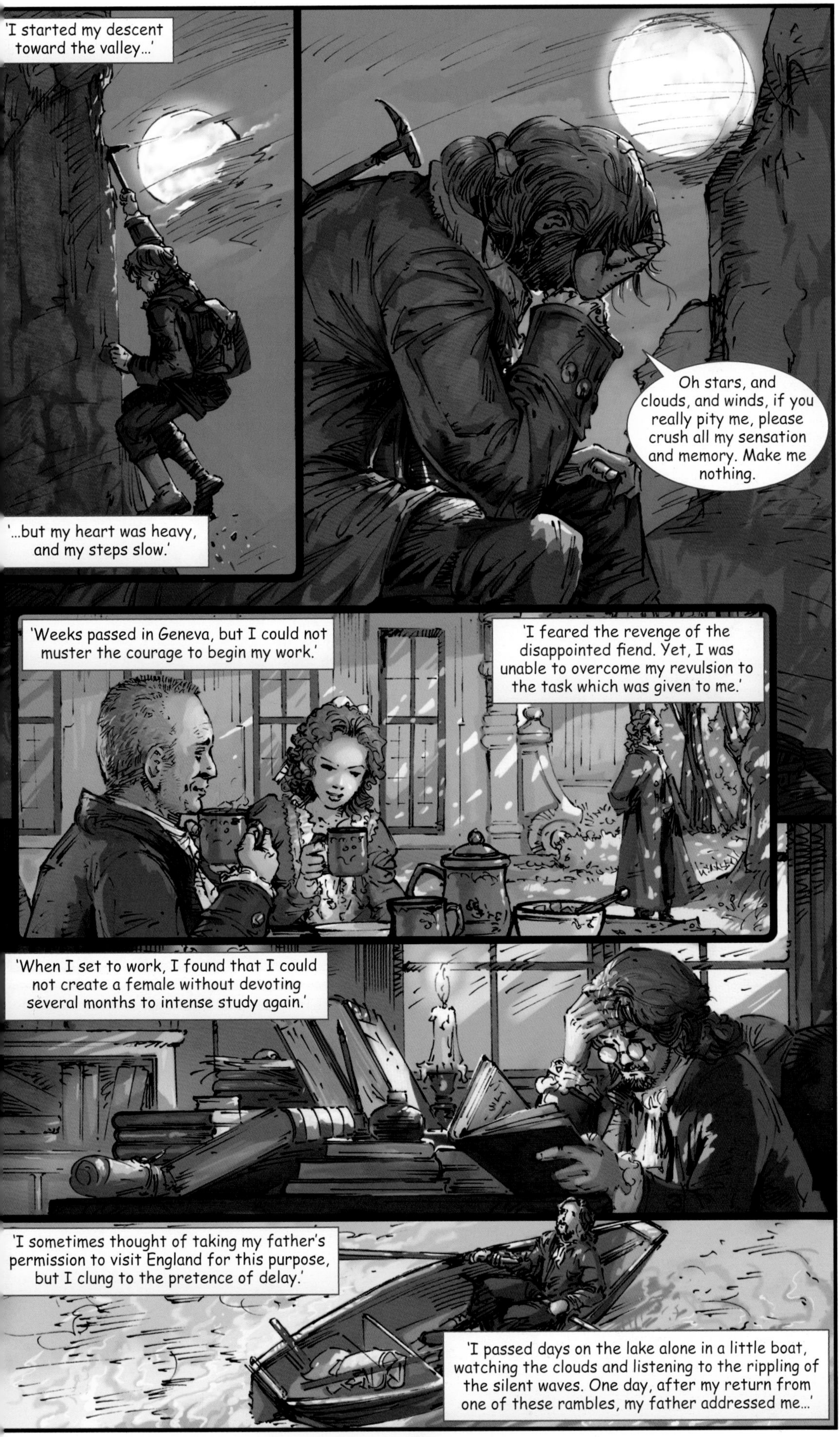
'I started my descent toward the valley...'
'...but my heart was heavy, and my steps slow.'
Oh stars, and clouds, and winds, if you really pity me, please crush all my sensation and memory. Make me nothing.
'Weeks passed in Geneva, but I could not muster the courage to begin my work.'
'I feared the revenge of the disappointed fiend. Yet, I was unable to overcome my revulsion to the task which was given to me.'
'When I set to work, I found that I could not create a female without devoting several months to intense study again.'
'I sometimes thought of taking my father's permission to visit England for this purpose, but I clung to the pretence of delay.'
'I passed days on the lake alone in a little boat, watching the clouds and listening to the rippling of the silent waves. One day, after my return from one of these rambles, my father addressed me...'

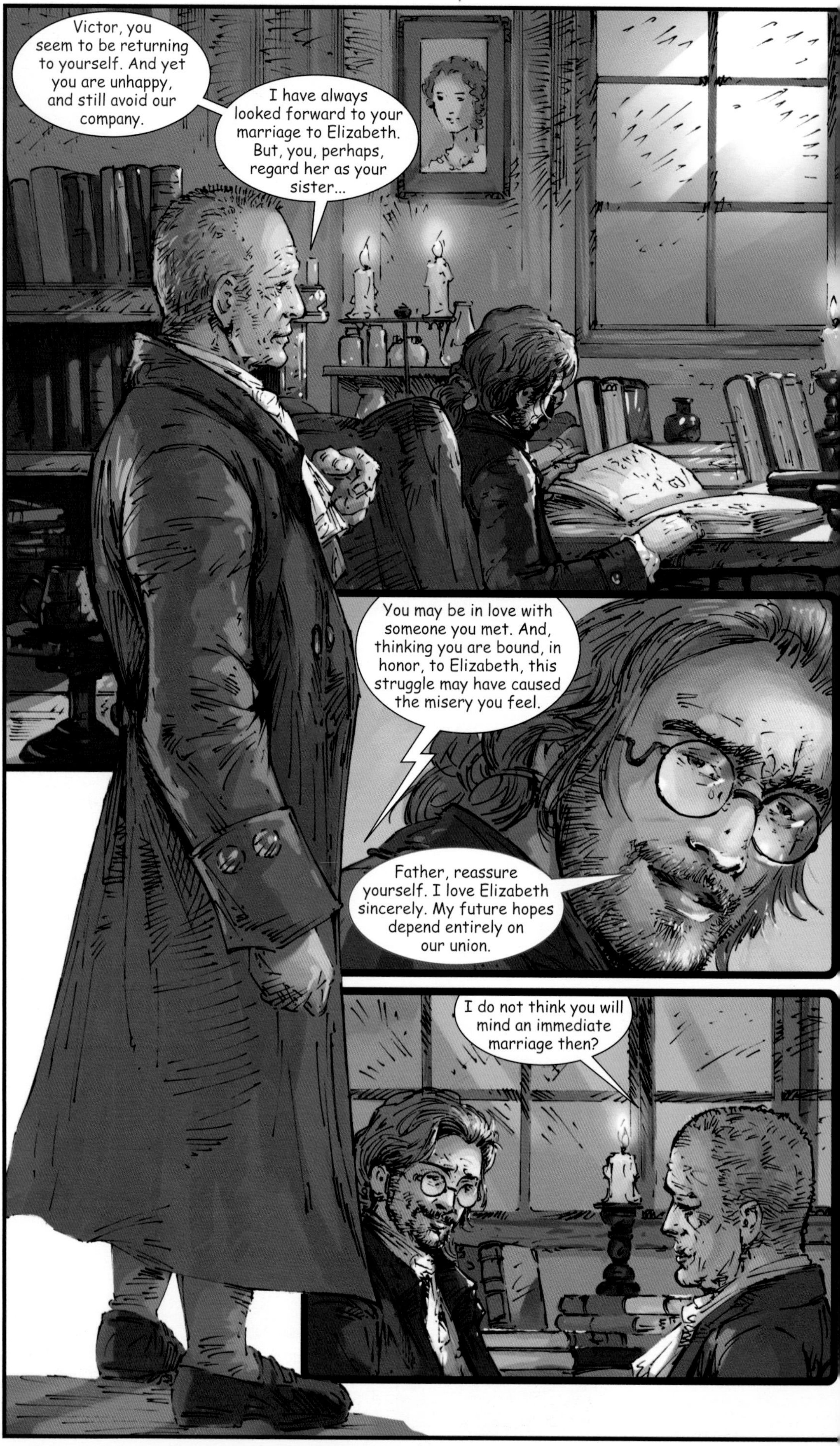
Victor, you seem to be returning to yourself. And yet you are unhappy, and still avoid our company.
I have always looked forward to your marriage to Elizabeth. But, you, perhaps, regard her as your sister...
You may be in love with someone you met. And, thinking you are bound, in honor, to Elizabeth, this struggle may have caused the misery you feel.
Father, reassure yourself. I love Elizabeth sincerely. My future hopes depend entirely on our union.
I do not think you will mind an immediate marriage then?

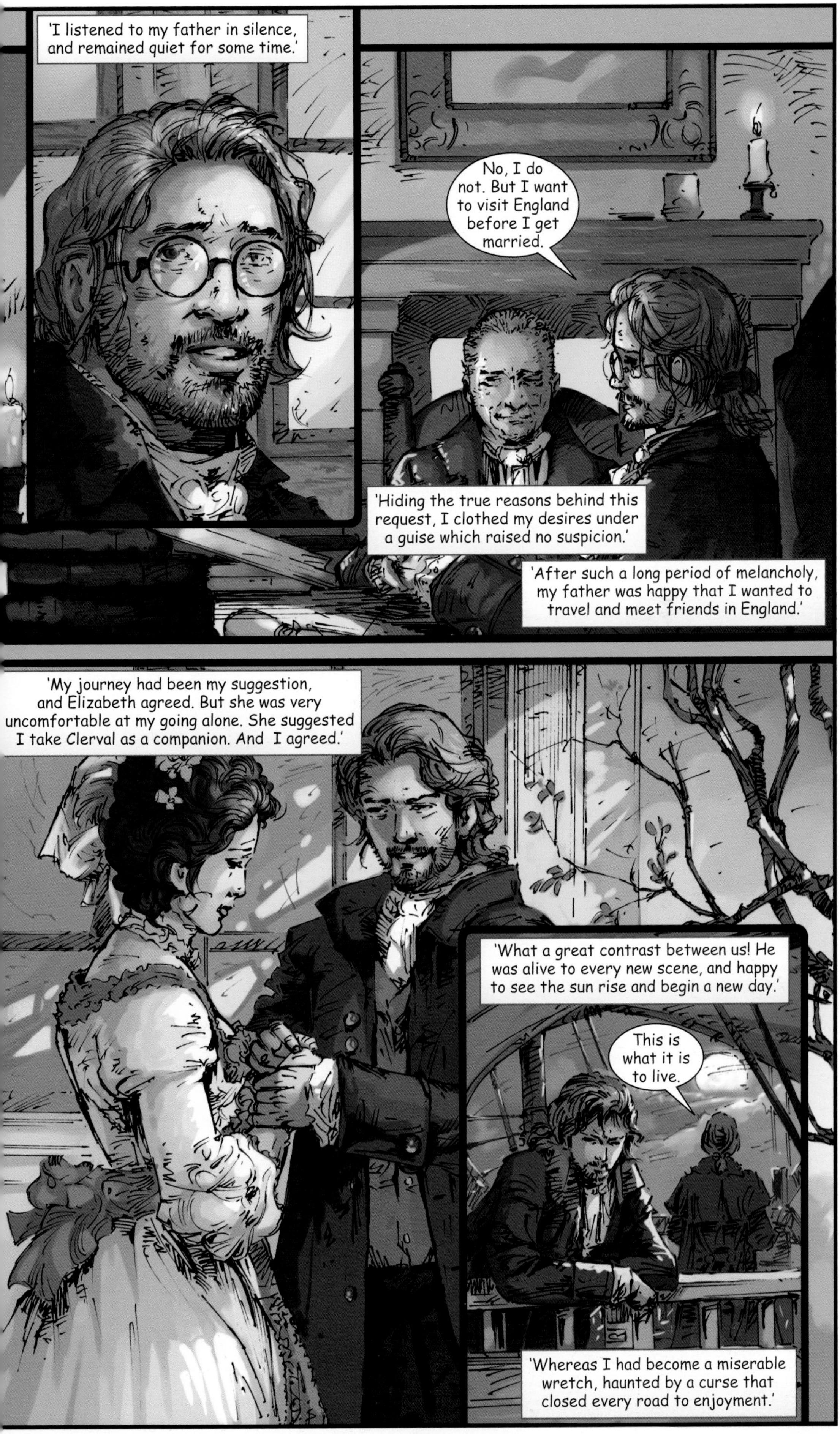
'I listened to my father in silence, and remained quiet for some time.'
No, I do not. But I want to visit England before I get married.
'Hiding the true reasons behind this request, I clothed my desires under a guise which raised no suspicion.'
'After such a long period of melancholy, my father was happy that I wanted to travel and meet friends in England.'
'My journey had been my suggestion, and Elizabeth agreed. But she was very uncomfortable at my going alone. She suggested I take Clerval as a companion. And I agreed.'
'What a great contrast between us! He was alive to every new scene, and happy to see the sun rise and begin a new day.'
This is what it is to live.
'Whereas I had become a miserable wretch, haunted by a curse that closed every road to enjoyment.'

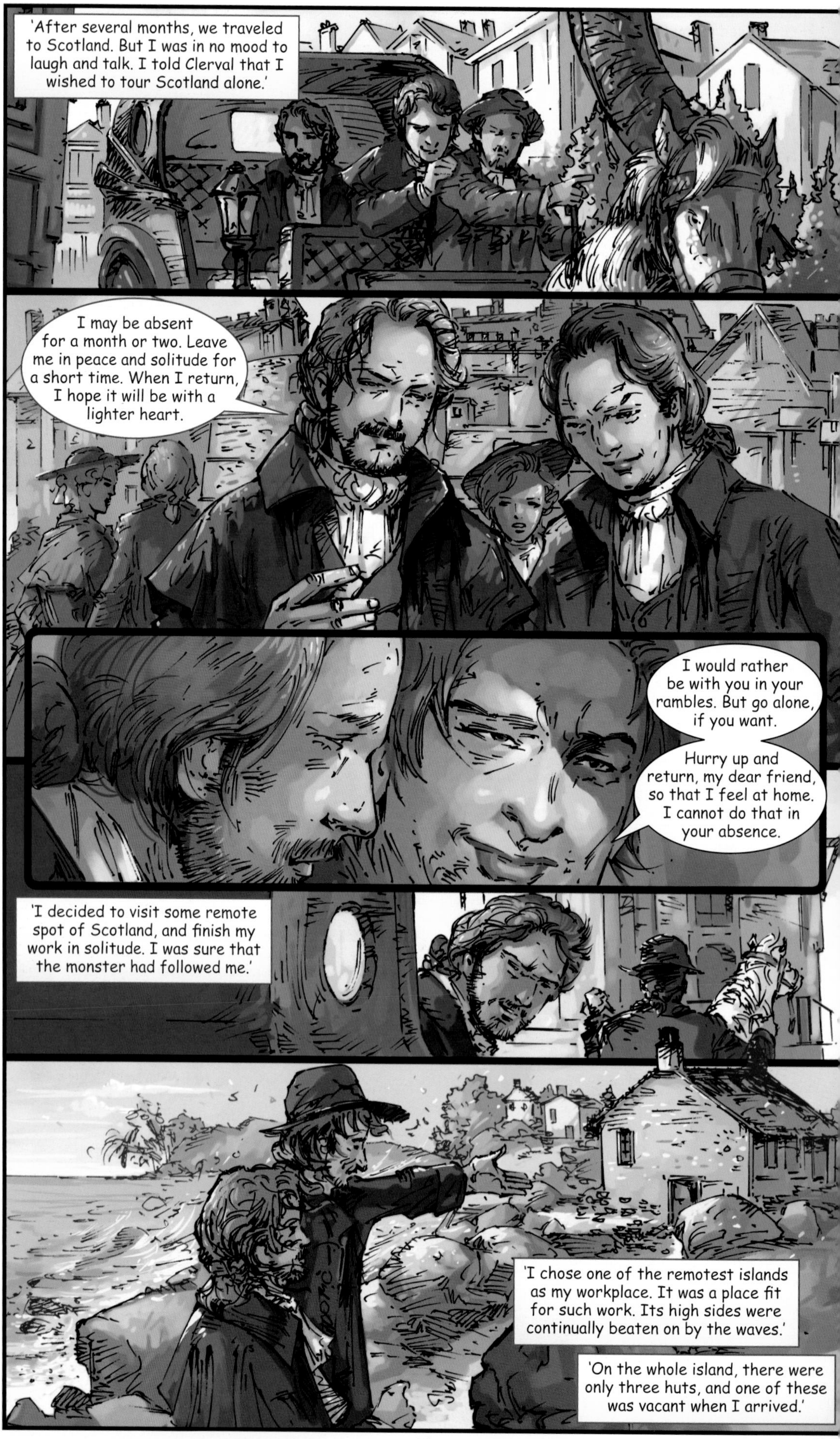
'After several months, we traveled to Scotland. But I was in no mood to laugh and talk. I told Clerval that I wished to tour Scotland alone.'
I may be absent for a month or two. Leave me in peace and solitude for a short time. When I return, I hope it will be with a lighter heart.
I would rather be with you in your rambles. But go alone, if you want.
Hurry up and return, my dear friend, so that I feel at home. I cannot do that in your absence.
'I decided to visit some remote spot of Scotland, and finish my work in solitude. I was sure that the monster had followed me.'
'I chose one of the remotest islands as my workplace. It was a place fit for such work. Its high sides were continually beaten on by the waves.'
'On the whole island, there were only three huts, and one of these was vacant when I arrived.'

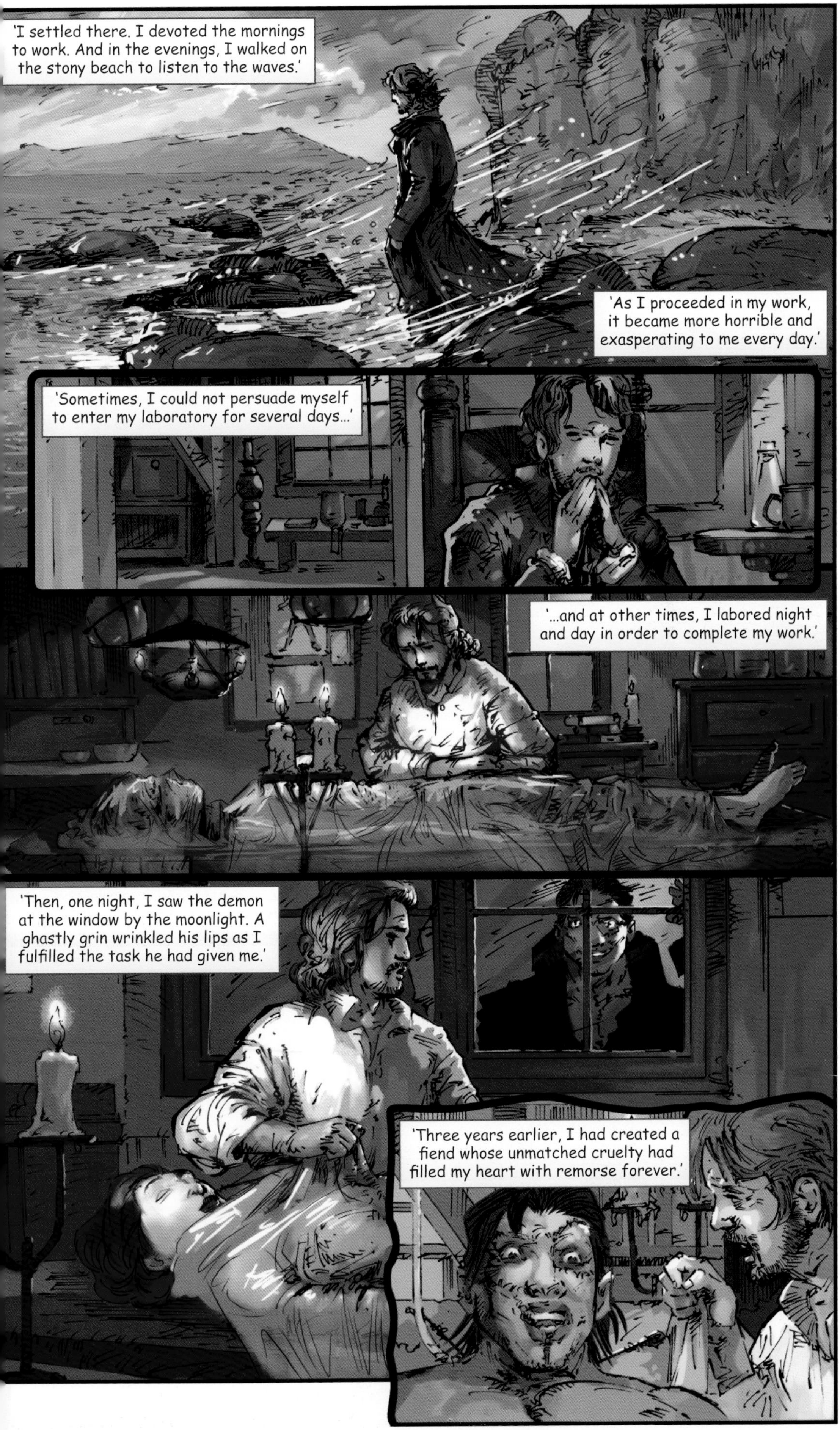
'I settled there. I devoted the mornings to work. And in the evenings, I walked on the stony beach to listen to the waves.'
'As I proceeded in my work, it became more horrible and exasperating to me every day.'
'Sometimes, I could not persuade myself to enter my laboratory for several days...'
'...and at other times, I labored night and day in order to complete my work.'
'Then, one night, I saw the demon at the window by the moonlight. A ghastly grin wrinkled his lips as I fulfilled the task he had given me.'
'Three years earlier, I had created a fiend whose unmatched cruelty had filled my heart with remorse forever.'

'I was now about to form another being, whose character I did not know. She might be ten thousand times more evil than her mate, and take even more pleasure in murder and wretchedness.'

'They might even hate each other.'

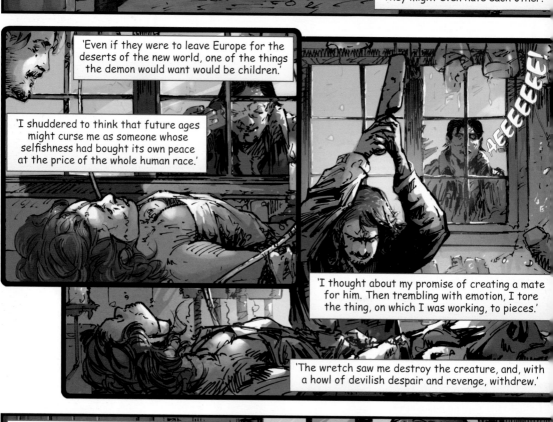

'Even if they were to leave Europe for the deserts of the new world, one of the things the demon would want would be children.'

'I shuddered to think that future ages might curse me as someone whose selfishness had bought its own peace at the price of the whole human race.'

AEEEEEE!

'I thought about my promise of creating a mate for him. Then trembling with emotion, I tore the thing, on which I was working, to pieces.'

'The wretch saw me destroy the creature, and, with a howl of devilish despair and revenge, withdrew.'

'I left the room and promised myself never to resume my work. With trembling steps, I walked toward my apartment.'

'A few minutes later, I heard the door creaking, as if someone had tried to open it softly.'

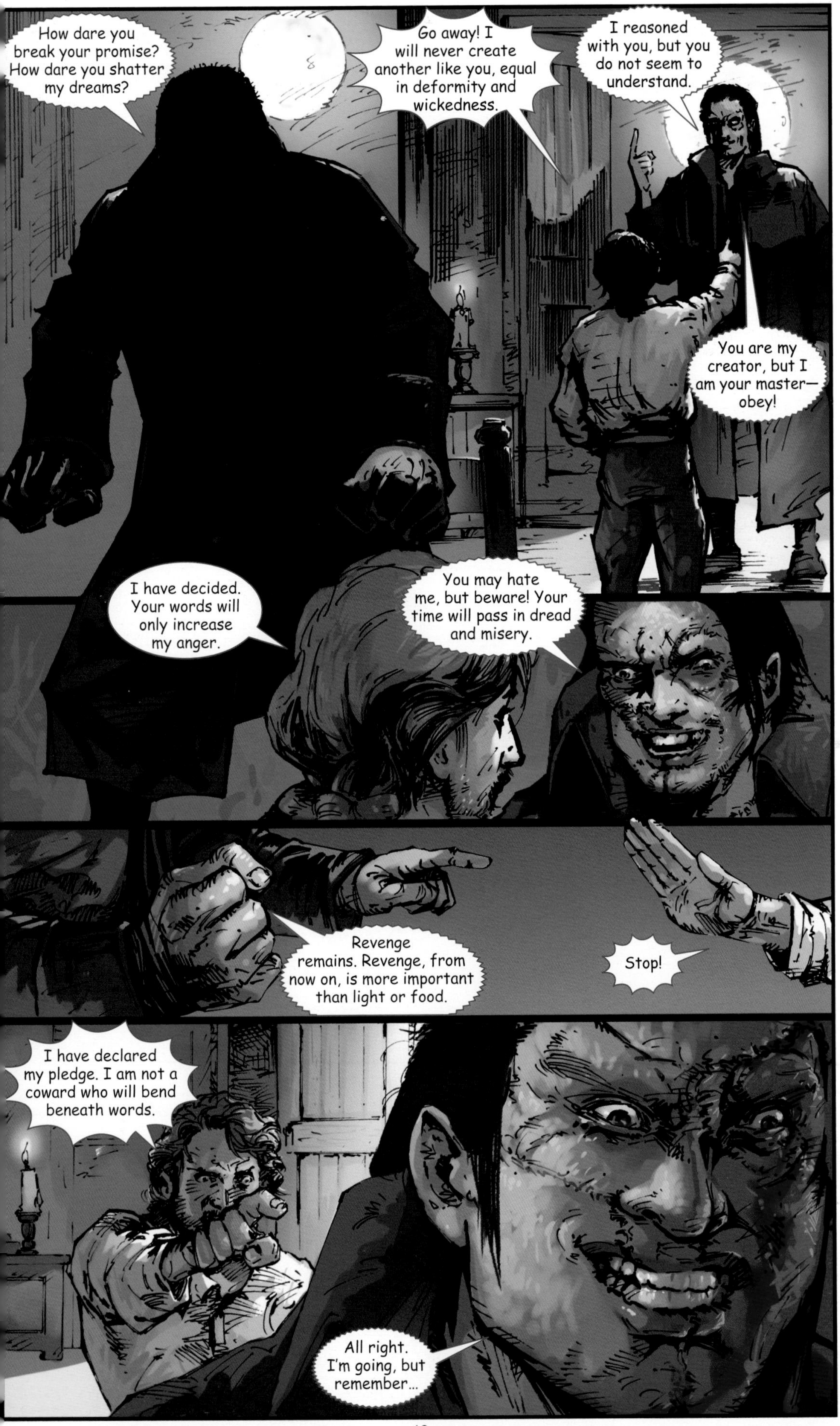
How dare you break your promise? How dare you shatter my dreams?
Go away! I will never create another like you, equal in deformity and wickedness.
I reasoned with you, but you do not seem to understand.
You are my creator, but I am your master—obey!
I have decided. Your words will only increase my anger.
You may hate me, but beware! Your time will pass in dread and misery.
Revenge remains. Revenge, from now on, is more important than light or food.
Stop!
I have declared my pledge. I am not a coward who will bend beneath words.
All right. I'm going, but remember...

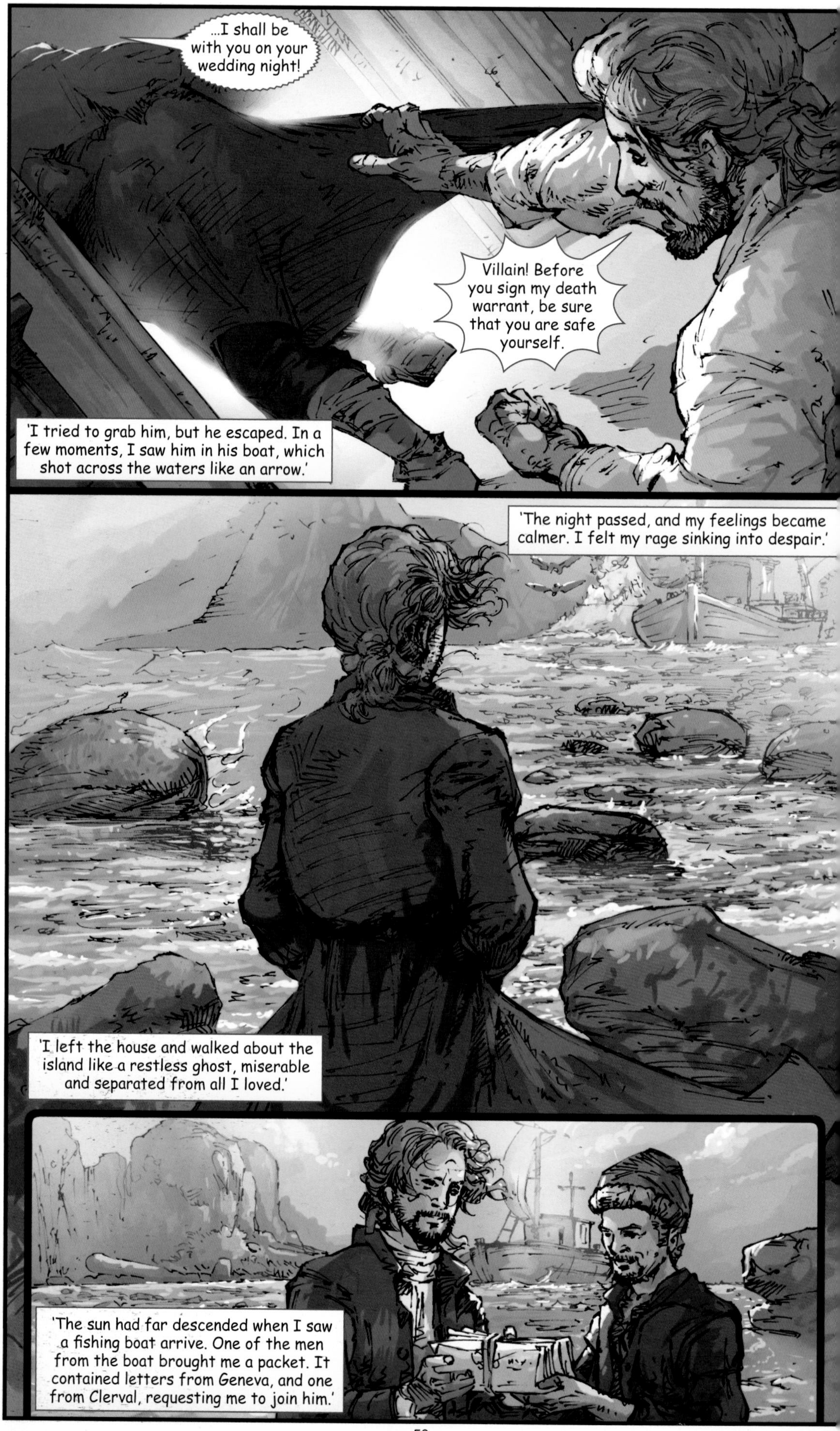
...I shall be with you on your wedding night!
Villain! Before you sign my death warrant, be sure that you are safe yourself.
'I tried to grab him, but he escaped. In a few moments, I saw him in his boat, which shot across the waters like an arrow.'
'The night passed, and my feelings became calmer. I felt my rage sinking into despair.'
'I left the house and walked about the island like a restless ghost, miserable and separated from all I loved.'
'The sun had far descended when I saw a fishing boat arrive. One of the men from the boat brought me a packet. It contained letters from Geneva, and one from Clerval, requesting me to join him.'

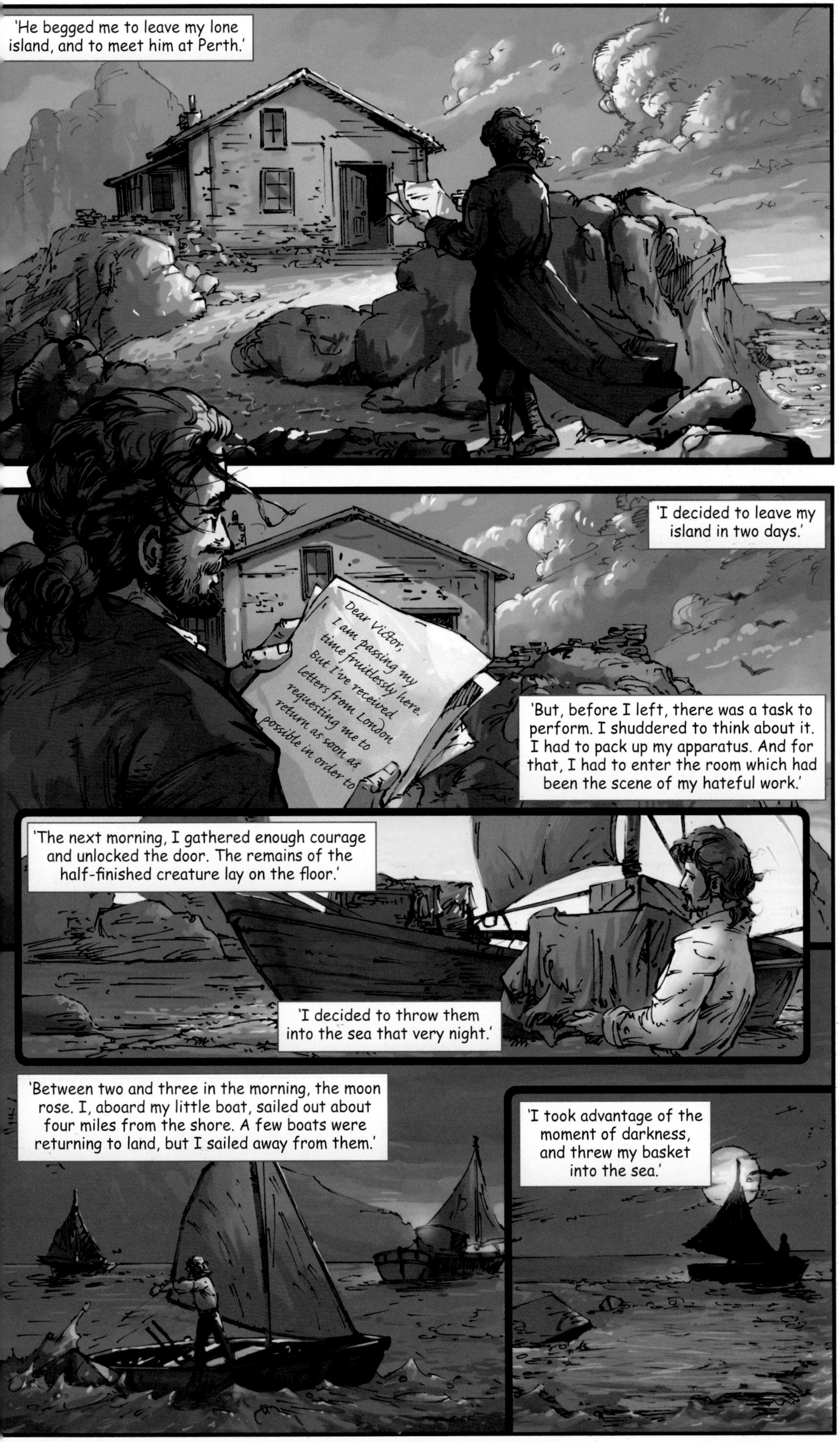
'He begged me to leave my lone island, and to meet him at Perth.'
'I decided to leave my island in two days.'
Dear Victor,
I am passing my time fruitlessly here. But I've received letters from London requesting me to return as soon as possible in order to
'But, before I left, there was a task to perform. I shuddered to think about it. I had to pack up my apparatus. And for that, I had to enter the room which had been the scene of my hateful work.'
'The next morning, I gathered enough courage and unlocked the door. The remains of the half-finished creature lay on the floor.'
'I decided to throw them into the sea that very night.'
'Between two and three in the morning, the moon rose. I, aboard my little boat, sailed out about four miles from the shore. A few boats were returning to land, but I sailed away from them.'
'I took advantage of the moment of darkness, and threw my basket into the sea.'

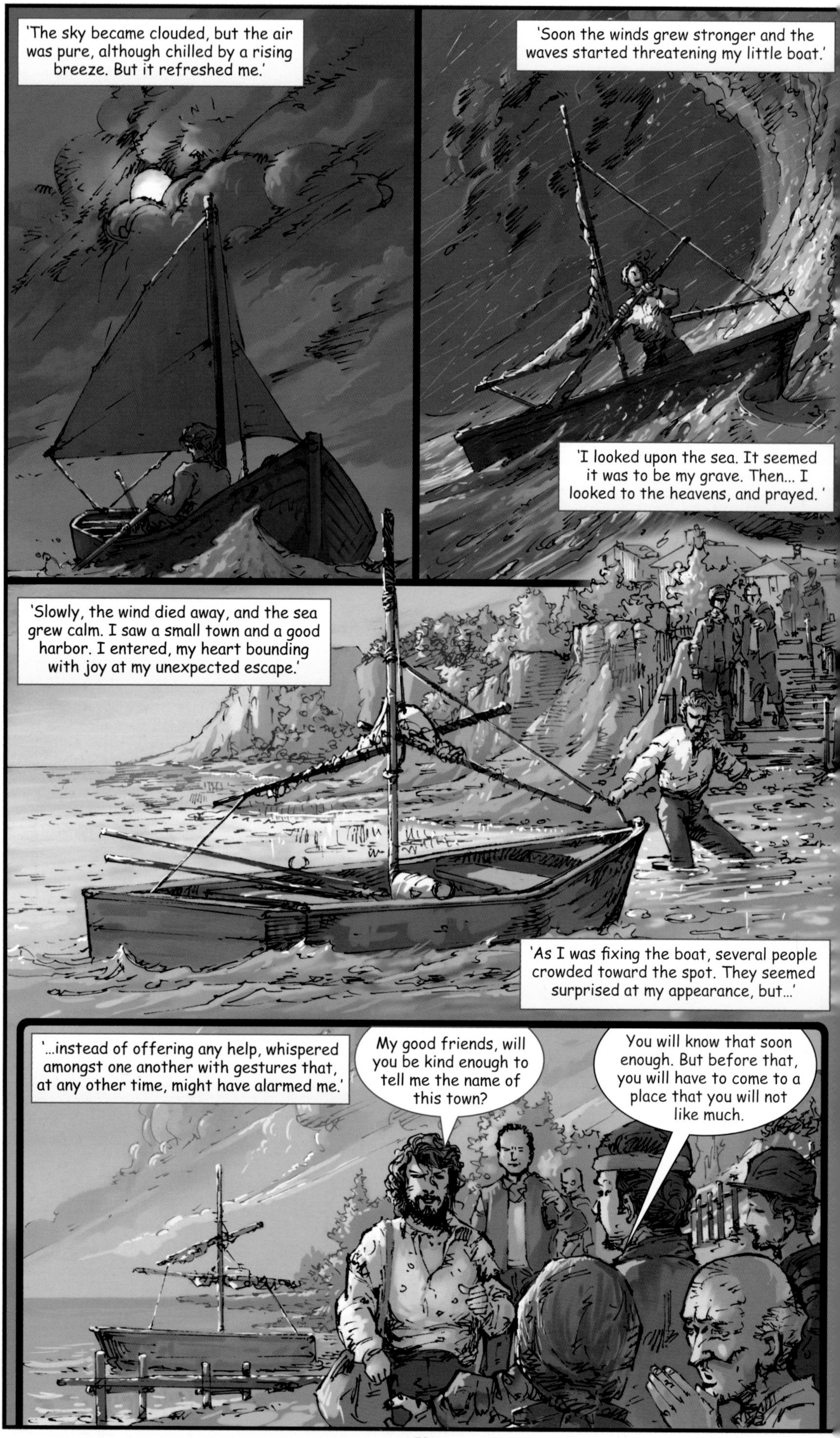
'The sky became clouded, but the air was pure, although chilled by a rising breeze. But it refreshed me.'
'Soon the winds grew stronger and the waves started threatening my little boat.'
'I looked upon the sea. It seemed it was to be my grave. Then... I looked to the heavens, and prayed.'
'Slowly, the wind died away, and the sea grew calm. I saw a small town and a good harbor. I entered, my heart bounding with joy at my unexpected escape.'
'As I was fixing the boat, several people crowded toward the spot. They seemed surprised at my appearance, but...'
'...instead of offering any help, whispered amongst one another with gestures that, at any other time, might have alarmed me.'
My good friends, will you be kind enough to tell me the name of this town?
You will know that soon enough. But before that, you will have to come to a place that you will not like much.

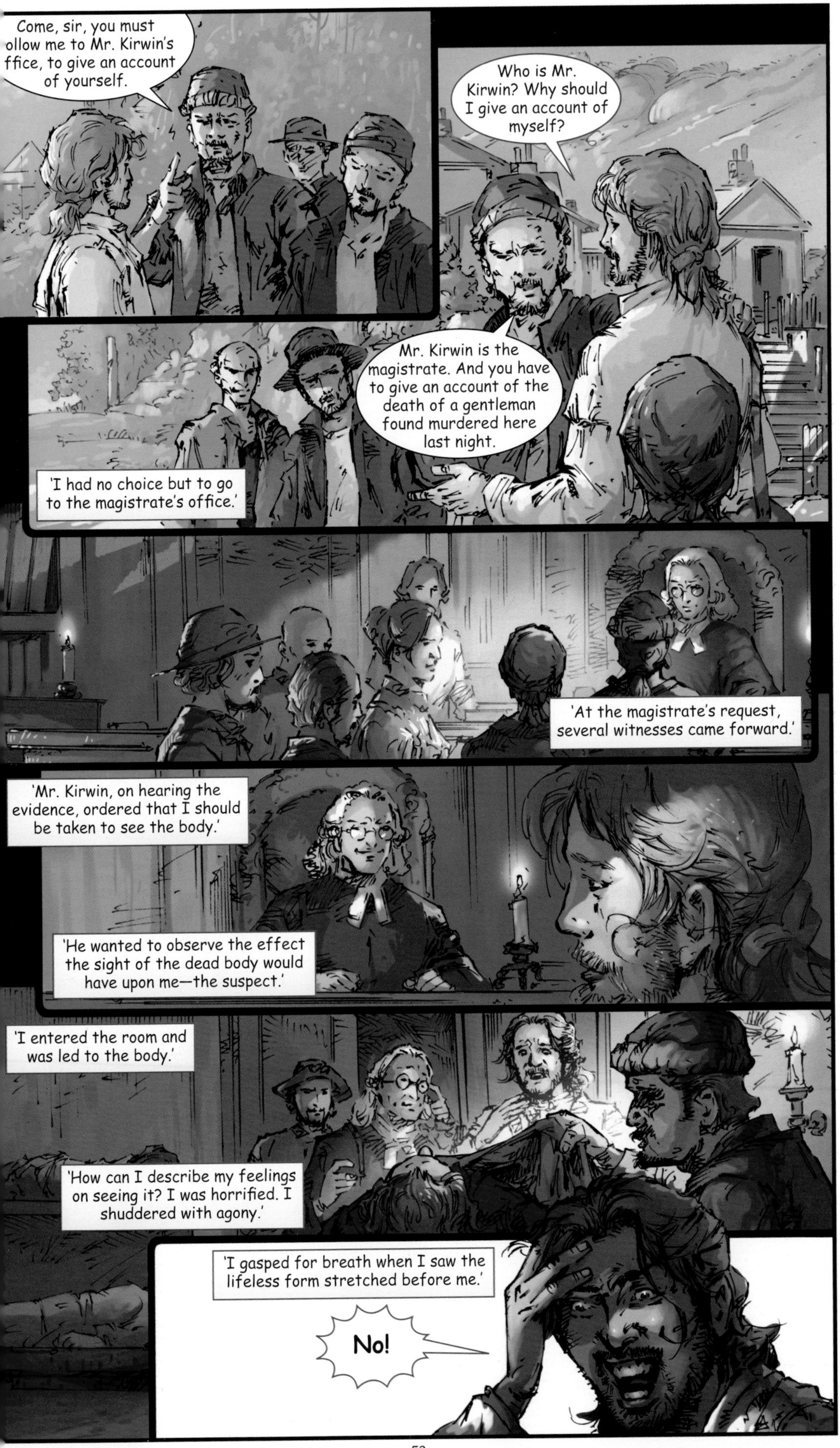

Come, sir, you must ollow me to Mr. Kirwin's ffice, to give an account of yourself.
Who is Mr. Kirwin? Why should I give an account of myself?
Mr. Kirwin is the magistrate. And you have to give an account of the death of a gentleman found murdered here last night.
'I had no choice but to go to the magistrate's office.'
'At the magistrate's request, several witnesses came forward.'
'Mr. Kirwin, on hearing the evidence, ordered that I should be taken to see the body.'
'He wanted to observe the effect the sight of the dead body would have upon me—the suspect.'
'I entered the room and was led to the body.'
'How can I describe my feelings on seeing it? I was horrified. I shuddered with agony.'
'I gasped for breath when I saw the lifeless form stretched before me.'
No!

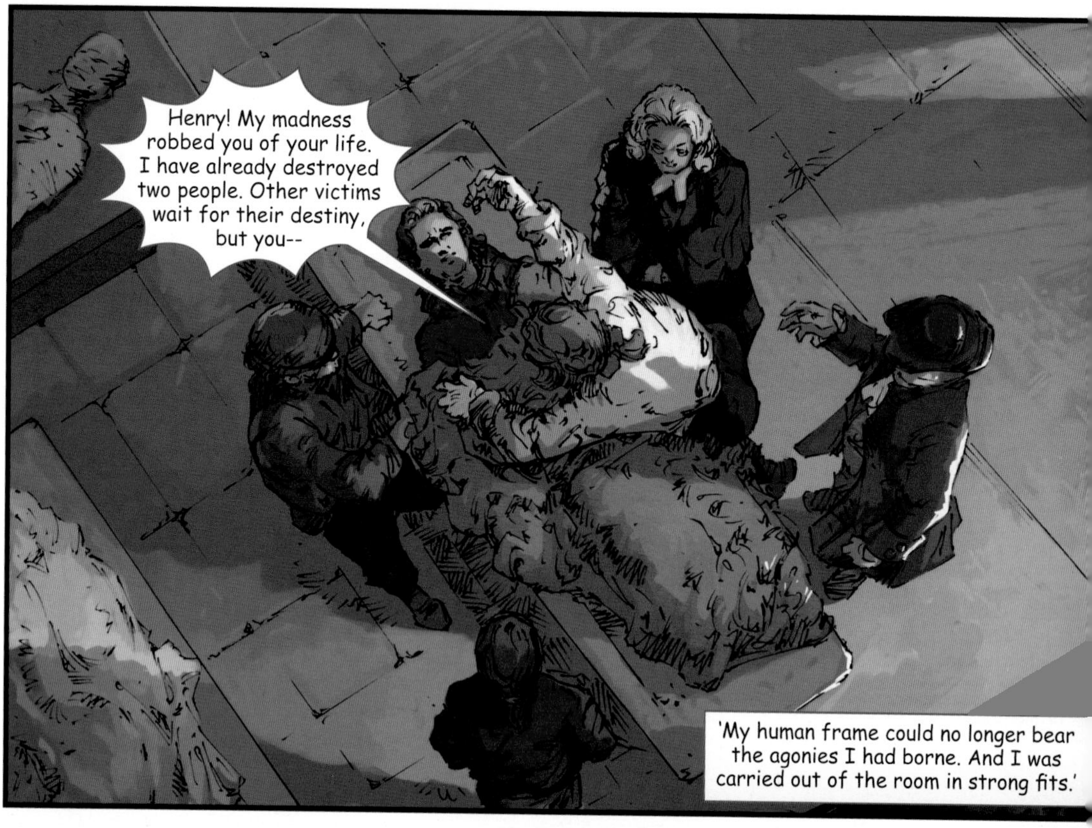
Henry! My madness robbed you of your life. I have already destroyed two people. Other victims wait for their destiny, but you--
'My human frame could no longer bear the agonies I had borne. And I was carried out of the room in strong fits.'

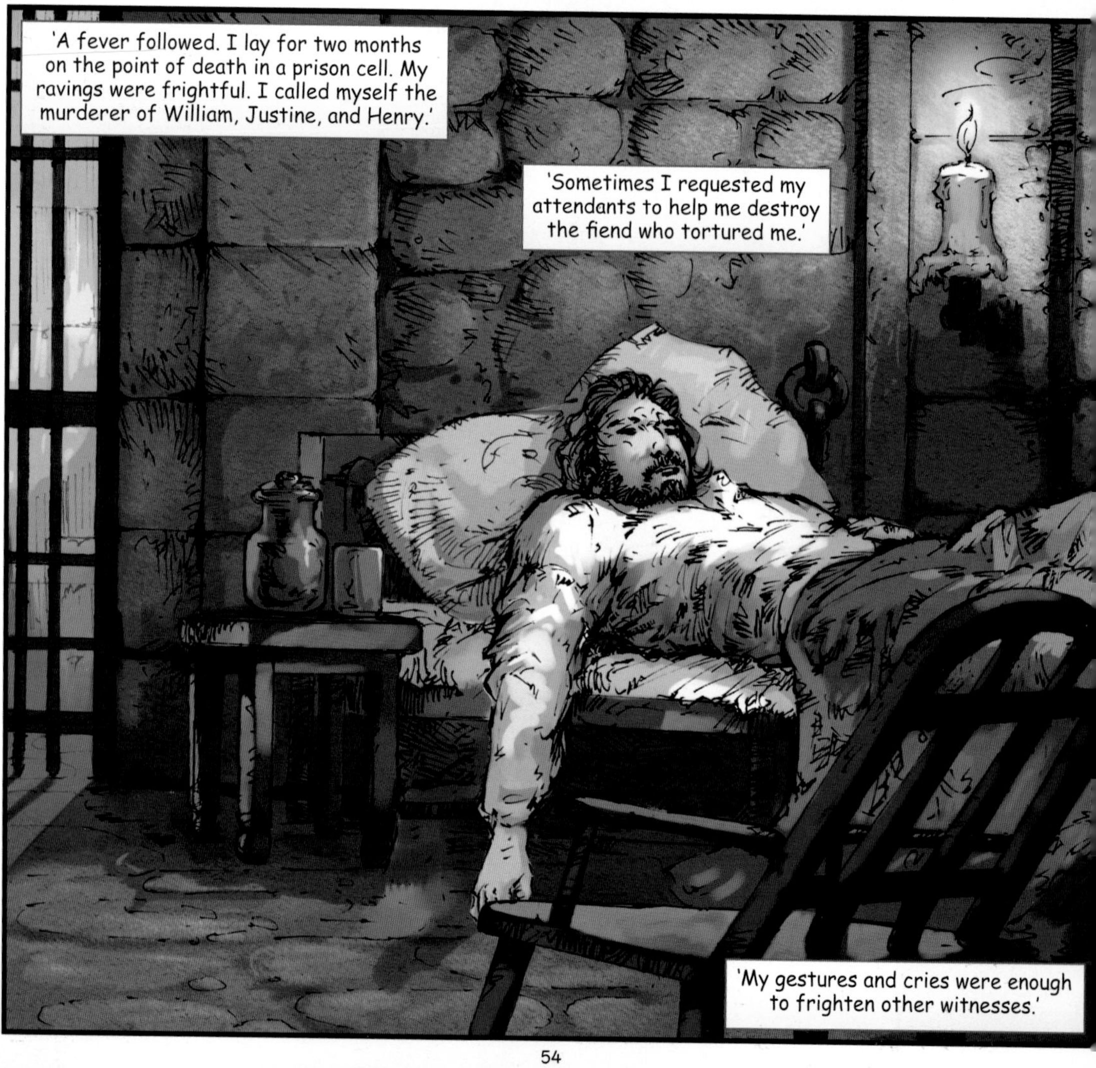
'A fever followed. I lay for two months on the point of death in a prison cell. My ravings were frightful. I called myself the murderer of William, Justine, and Henry.'
'Sometimes I requested my attendants to help me destroy the fiend who tortured me.'
'My gestures and cries were enough to frighten other witnesses.'

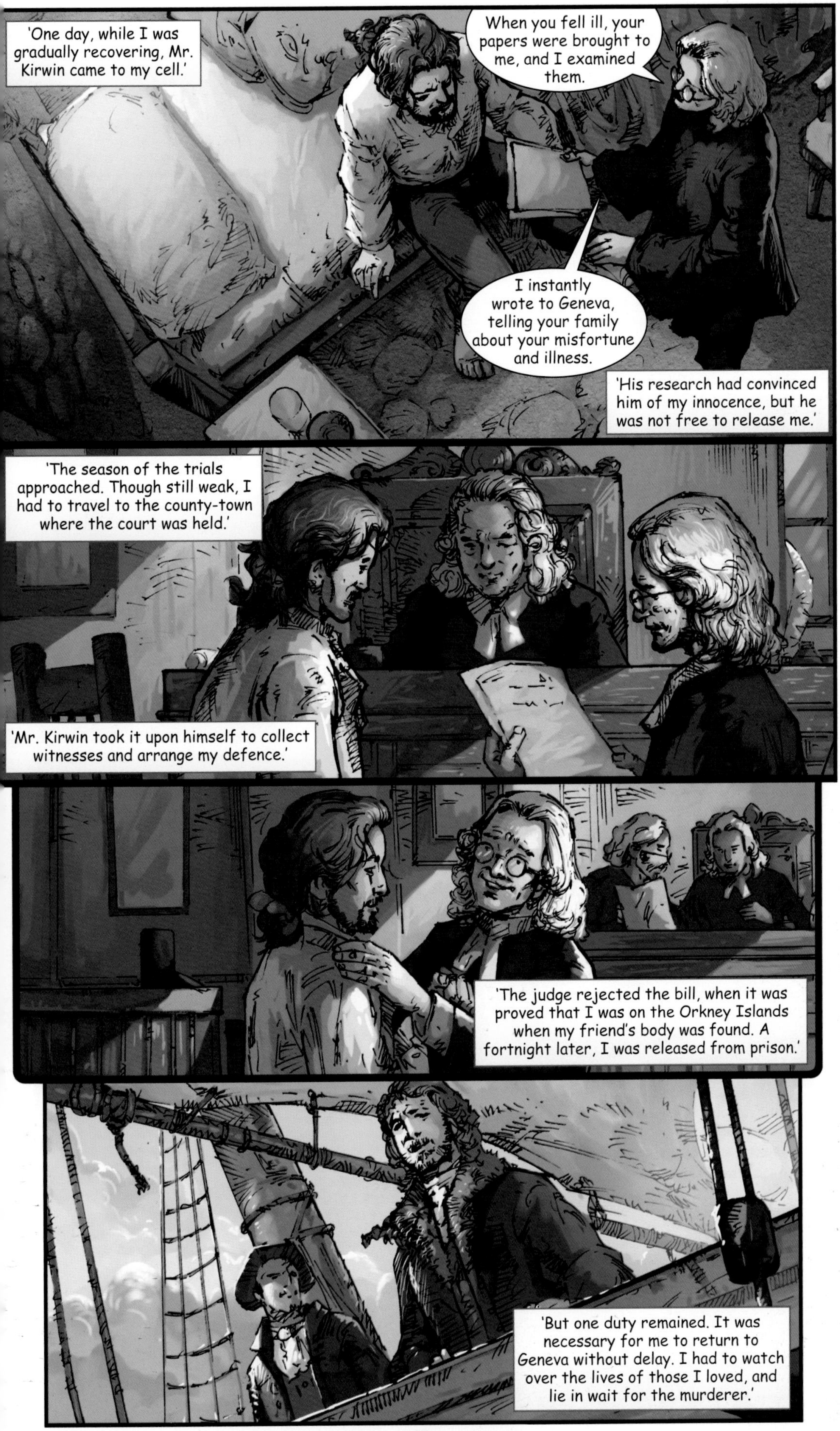
'One day, while I was gradually recovering, Mr. Kirwin came to my cell.'
When you fell ill, your papers were brought to me, and I examined them.
I instantly wrote to Geneva, telling your family about your misfortune and illness.
'His research had convinced him of my innocence, but he was not free to release me.'
'The season of the trials approached. Though still weak, I had to travel to the county-town where the court was held.'
'Mr. Kirwin took it upon himself to collect witnesses and arrange my defence.'
'The judge rejected the bill, when it was proved that I was on the Orkney Islands when my friend's body was found. A fortnight later, I was released from prison.'
'But one duty remained. It was necessary for me to return to Geneva without delay. I had to watch over the lives of those I loved, and lie in wait for the murderer.'

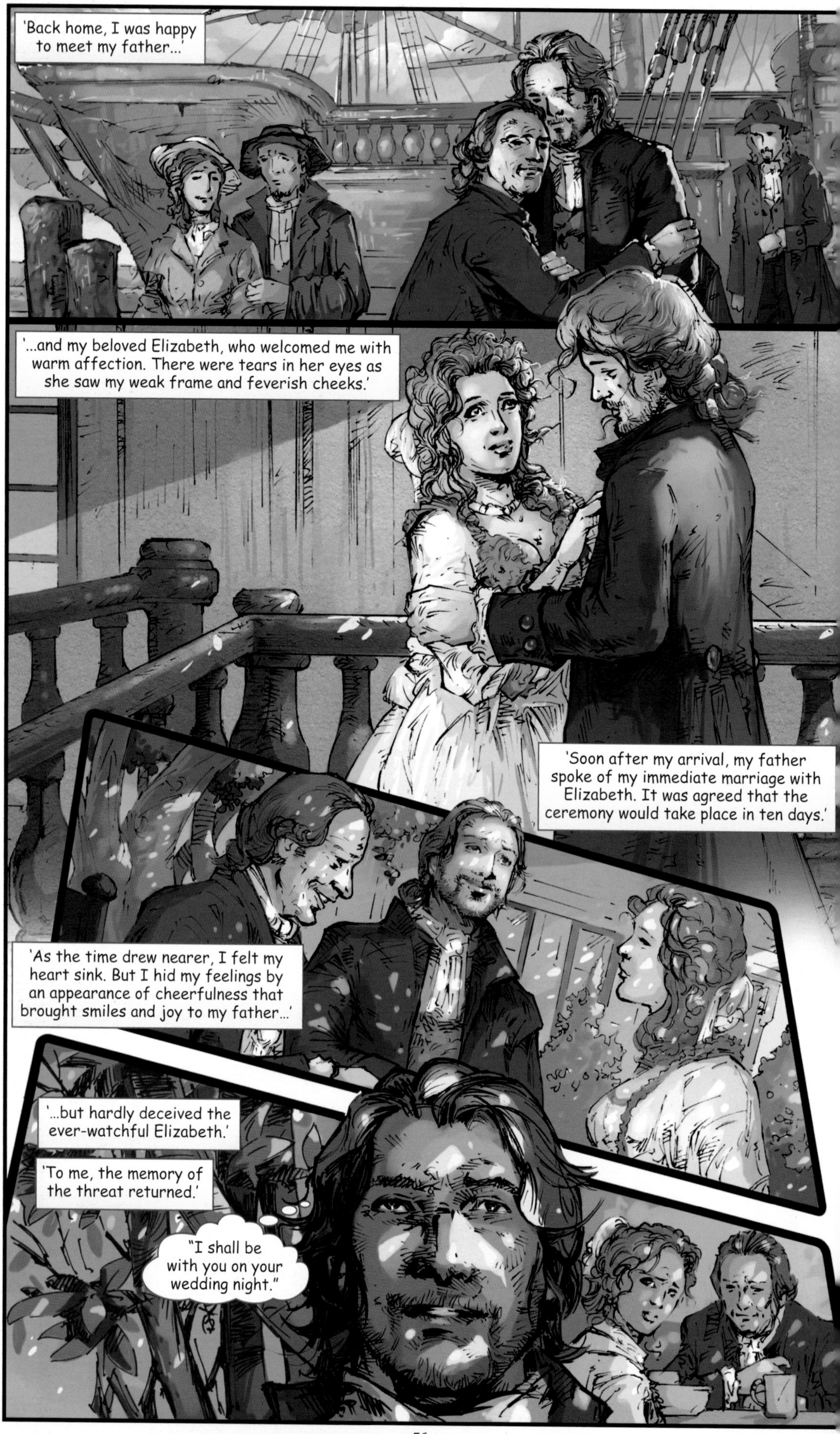
'Back home, I was happy to meet my father...'
'...and my beloved Elizabeth, who welcomed me with warm affection. There were tears in her eyes as she saw my weak frame and feverish cheeks.'
'Soon after my arrival, my father spoke of my immediate marriage with Elizabeth. It was agreed that the ceremony would take place in ten days.'
'As the time drew nearer, I felt my heart sink. But I hid my feelings by an appearance of cheerfulness that brought smiles and joy to my father...'
'...but hardly deceived the ever-watchful Elizabeth.'
'To me, the memory of the threat returned.'
"I shall be with you on your wedding night."

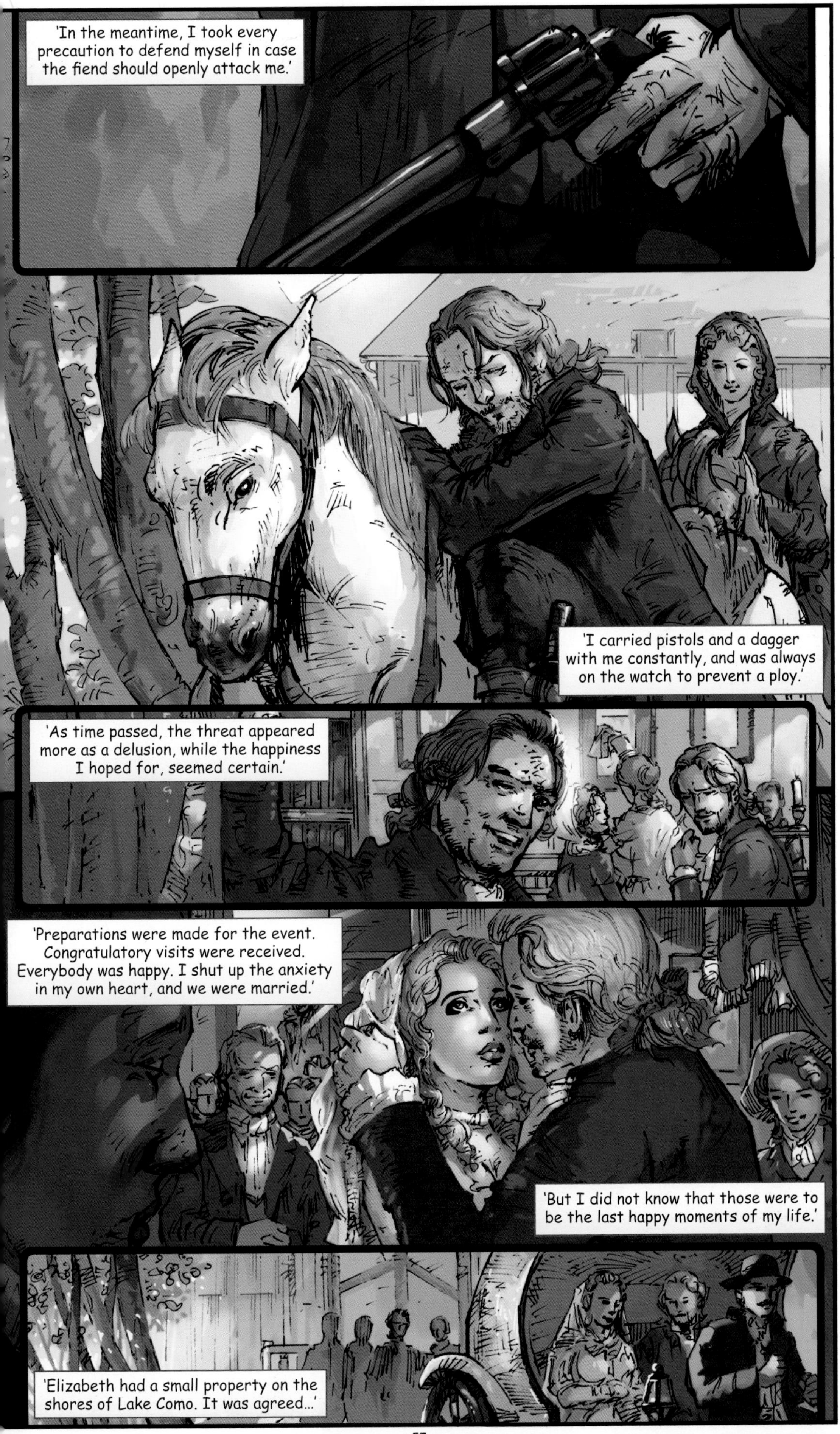
'In the meantime, I took every precaution to defend myself in case the fiend should openly attack me.'
'I carried pistols and a dagger with me constantly, and was always on the watch to prevent a ploy.'
'As time passed, the threat appeared more as a delusion, while the happiness I hoped for, seemed certain.'
'Preparations were made for the event. Congratulatory visits were received. Everybody was happy. I shut up the anxiety in my own heart, and we were married.'
'But I did not know that those were to be the last happy moments of my life.'
'Elizabeth had a small property on the shores of Lake Como. It was agreed...'

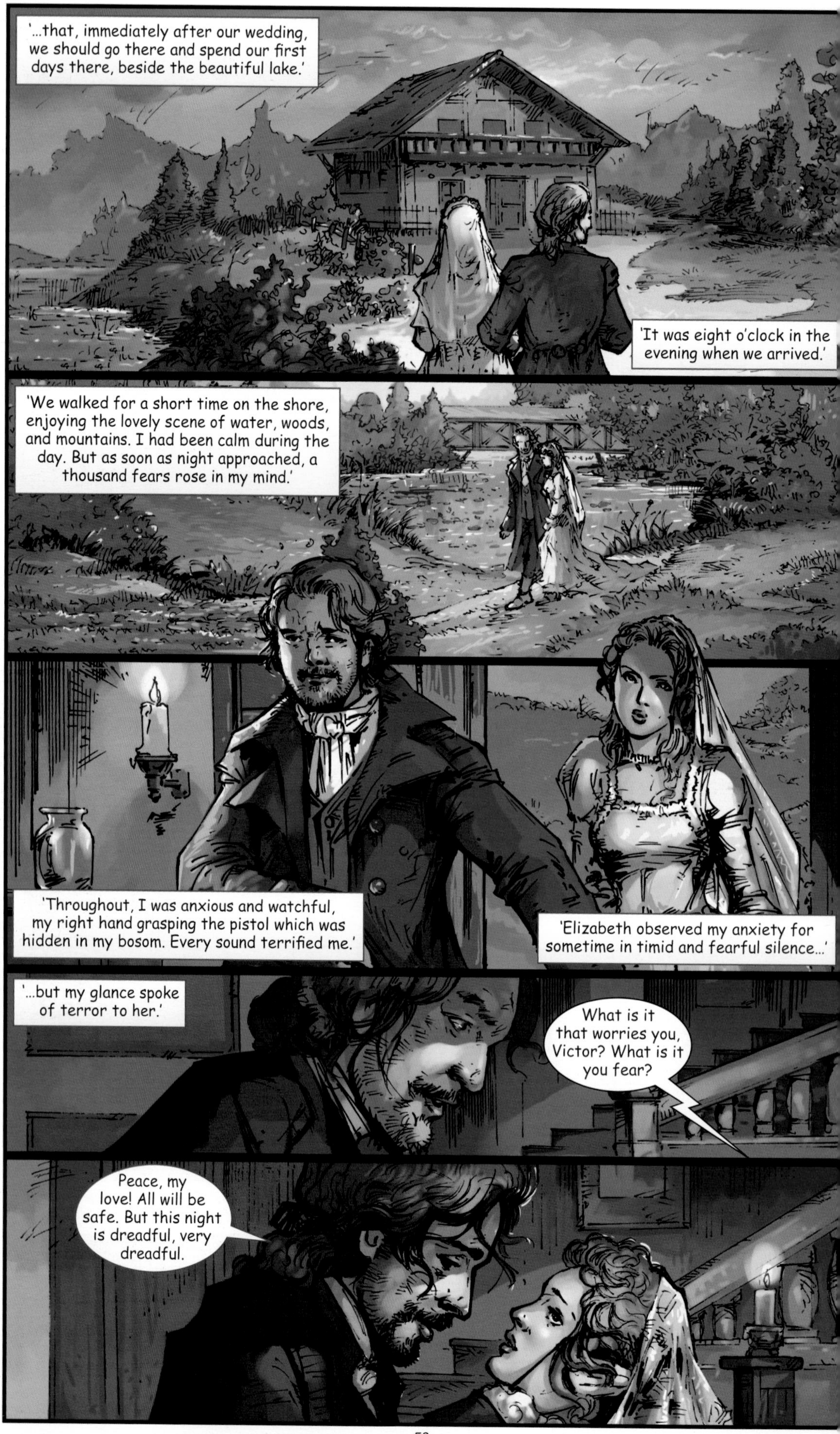
'...that, immediately after our wedding, we should go there and spend our first days there, beside the beautiful lake.'
'It was eight o'clock in the evening when we arrived.'
'We walked for a short time on the shore, enjoying the lovely scene of water, woods, and mountains. I had been calm during the day. But as soon as night approached, a thousand fears rose in my mind.'
'Throughout, I was anxious and watchful, my right hand grasping the pistol which was hidden in my bosom. Every sound terrified me.'
'Elizabeth observed my anxiety for sometime in timid and fearful silence...'
'...but my glance spoke of terror to her.'
What is it that worries you, Victor? What is it you fear?
Peace, my love! All will be safe. But this night is dreadful, very dreadful.

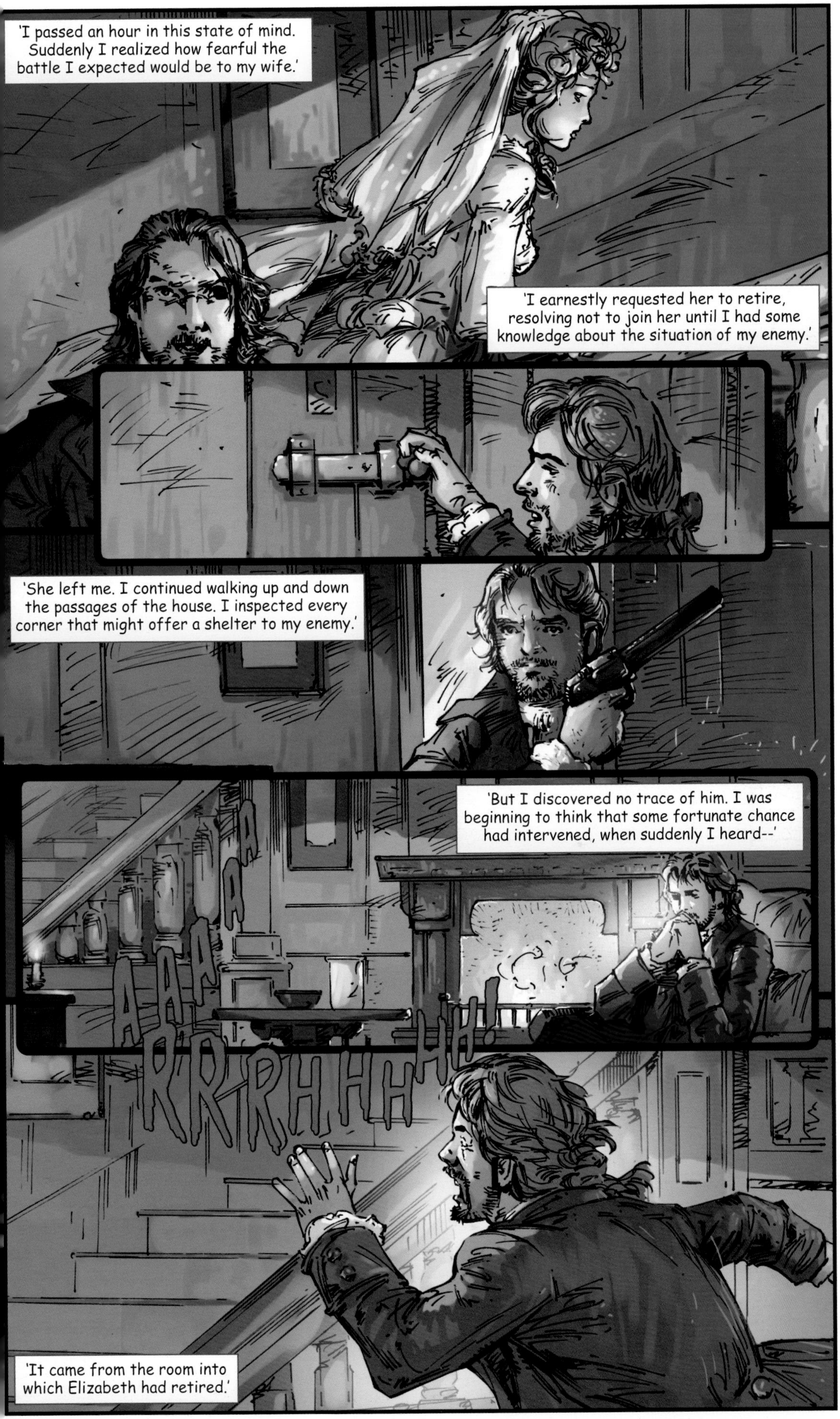
'I passed an hour in this state of mind. Suddenly I realized how fearful the battle I expected would be to my wife.'
'I earnestly requested her to retire, resolving not to join her until I had some knowledge about the situation of my enemy.'
'She left me. I continued walking up and down the passages of the house. I inspected every corner that might offer a shelter to my enemy.'
'But I discovered no trace of him. I was beginning to think that some fortunate chance had intervened, when suddenly I heard--'
AAAAAAARRRHHHHH!
'It came from the room into which Elizabeth had retired.'

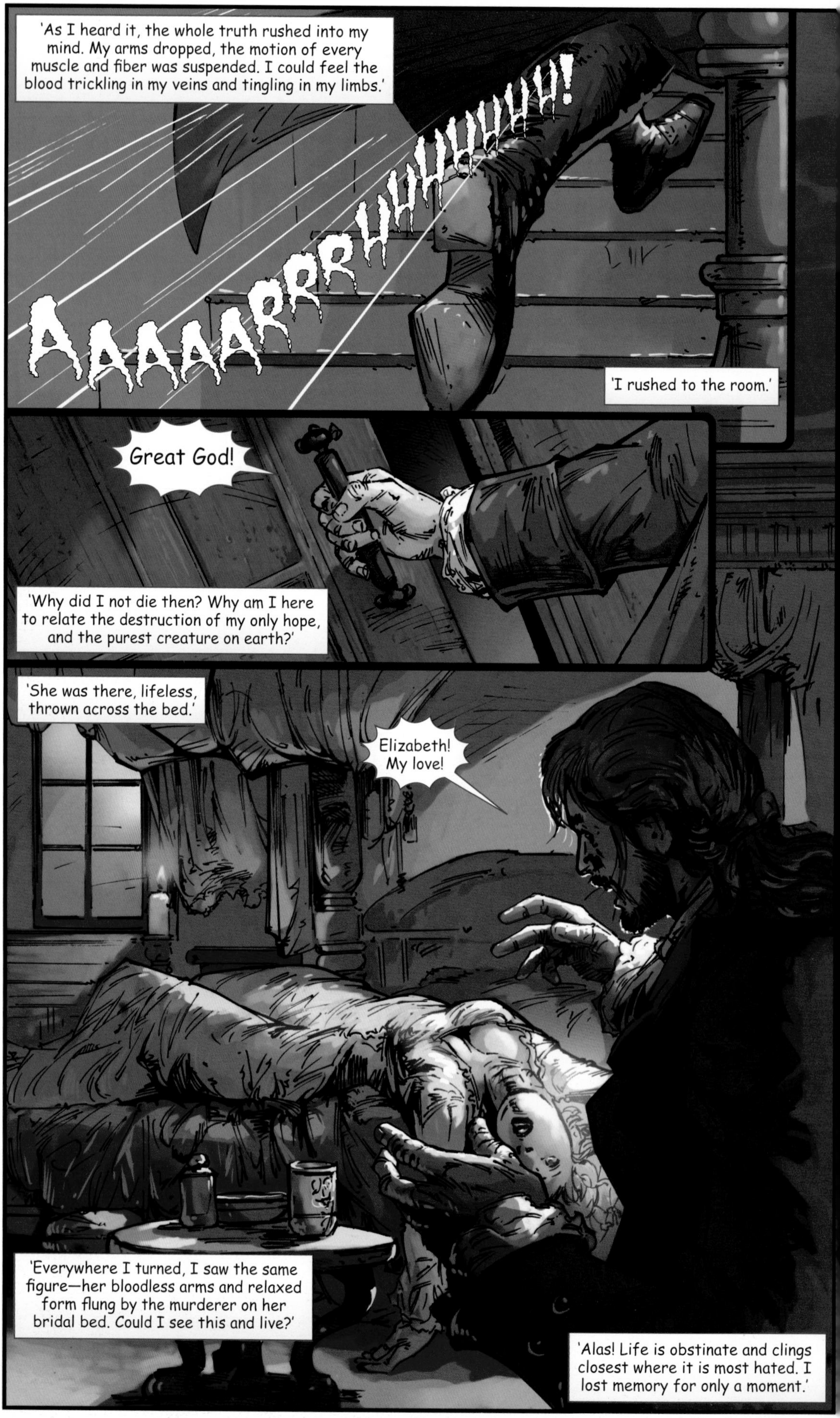
'As I heard it, the whole truth rushed into my mind. My arms dropped, the motion of every muscle and fiber was suspended. I could feel the blood trickling in my veins and tingling in my limbs.'
AAAAARRRRHHHHHHHH!
'I rushed to the room.'
Great God!
'Why did I not die then? Why am I here to relate the destruction of my only hope, and the purest creature on earth?'
'She was there, lifeless, thrown across the bed.'
Elizabeth! My love!
'Everywhere I turned, I saw the same figure—her bloodless arms and relaxed form flung by the murderer on her bridal bed. Could I see this and live?'
'Alas! Life is obstinate and clings closest where it is most hated. I lost memory for only a moment.'

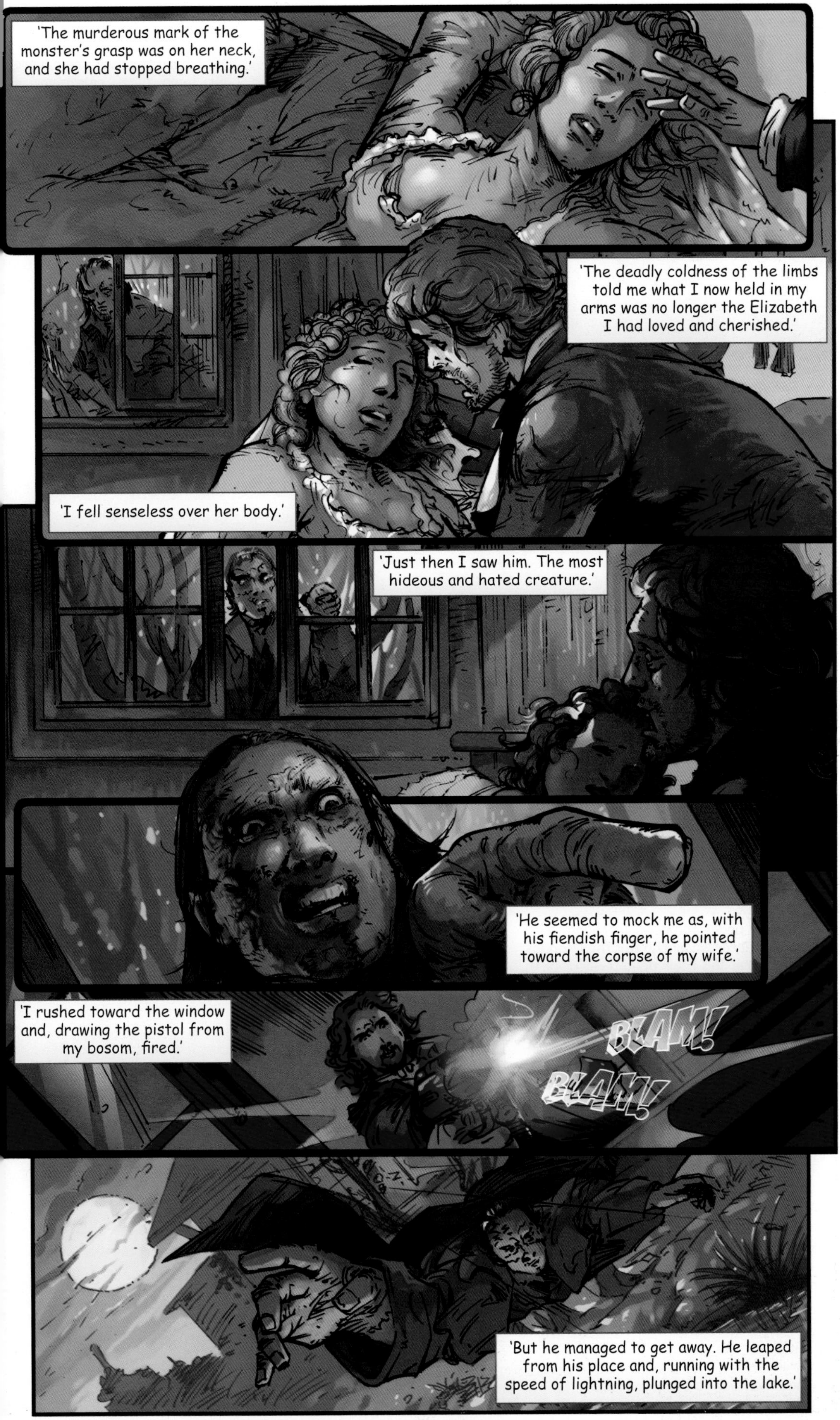
'The murderous mark of the monster's grasp was on her neck, and she had stopped breathing.'
'The deadly coldness of the limbs told me what I now held in my arms was no longer the Elizabeth I had loved and cherished.'
'I fell senseless over her body.'
'Just then I saw him. The most hideous and hated creature.'
'He seemed to mock me as, with his fiendish finger, he pointed toward the corpse of my wife.'
'I rushed toward the window and, drawing the pistol from my bosom, fired.'
BLAM!
BLAM!
'But he managed to get away. He leaped from his place and, running with the speed of lightning, plunged into the lake.'

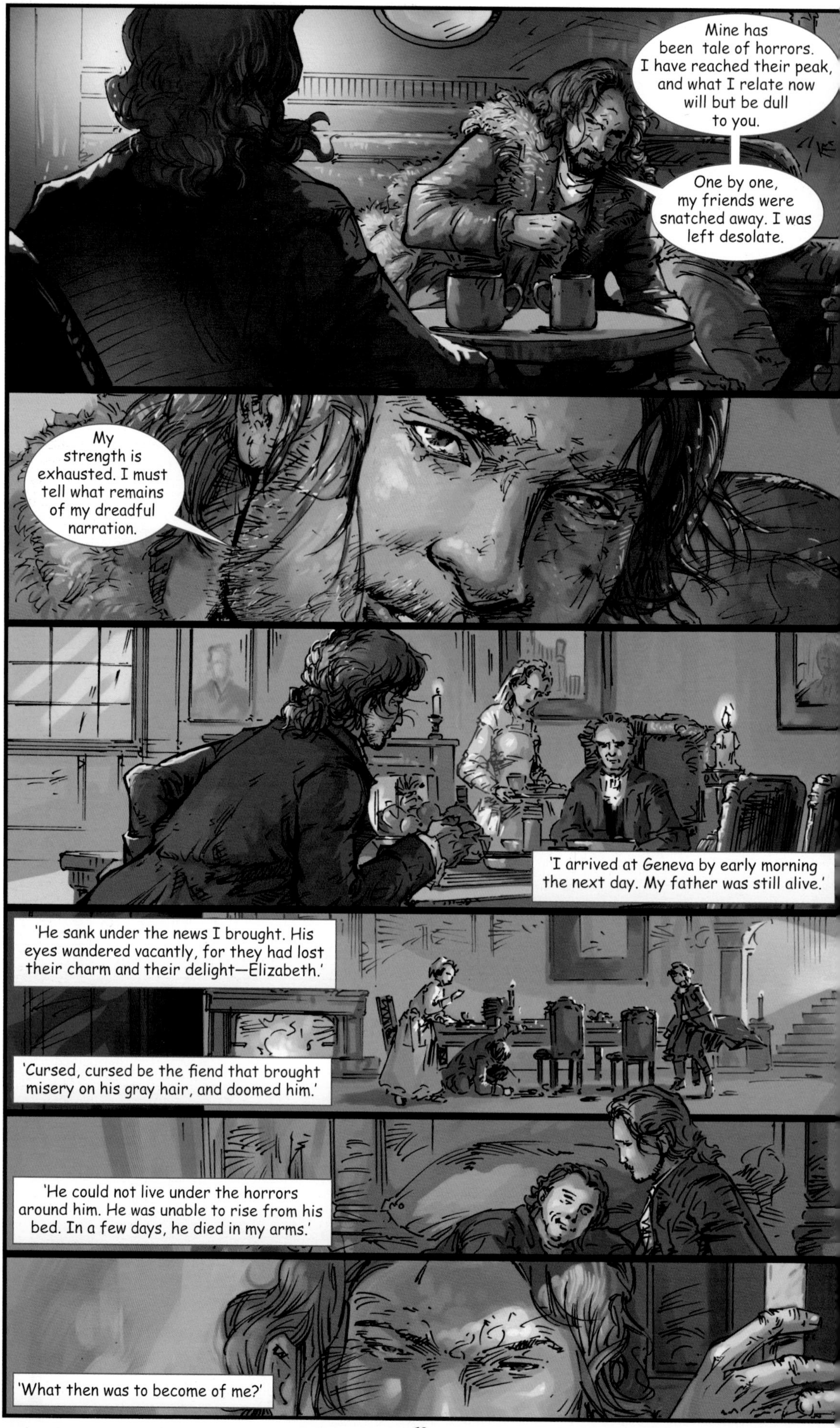
Mine has been tale of horrors. I have reached their peak, and what I relate now will but be dull to you.
One by one, my friends were snatched away. I was left desolate.
My strength is exhausted. I must tell what remains of my dreadful narration.
'I arrived at Geneva by early morning the next day. My father was still alive.'
'He sank under the news I brought. His eyes wandered vacantly, for they had lost their charm and their delight—Elizabeth.'
'Cursed, cursed be the fiend that brought misery on his gray hair, and doomed him.'
'He could not live under the horrors around him. He was unable to rise from his bed. In a few days, he died in my arms.'
'What then was to become of me?'

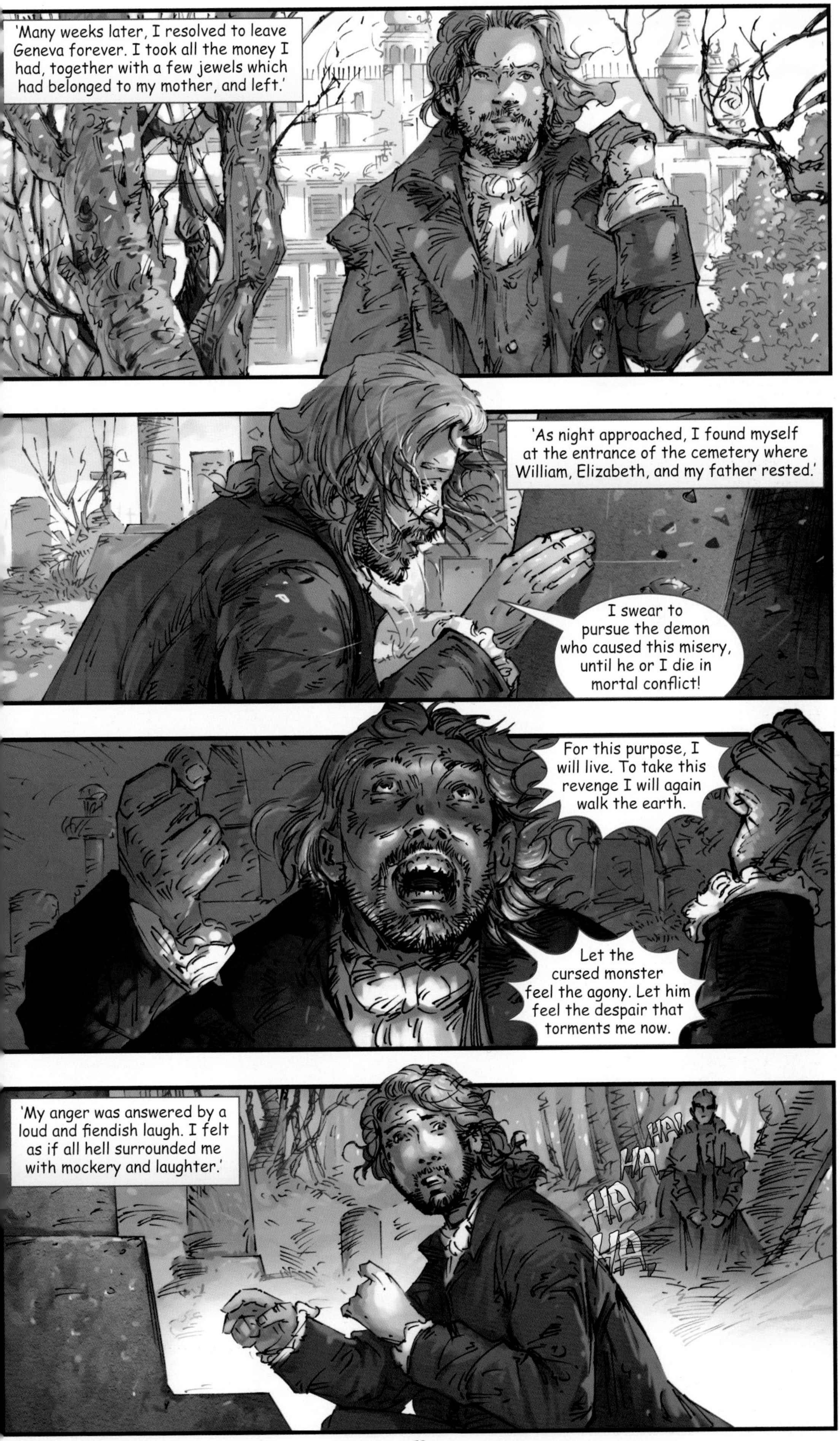
'Many weeks later, I resolved to leave Geneva forever. I took all the money I had, together with a few jewels which had belonged to my mother, and left.'
'As night approached, I found myself at the entrance of the cemetery where William, Elizabeth, and my father rested.'
I swear to pursue the demon who caused this misery, until he or I die in mortal conflict!
For this purpose, I will live. To take this revenge I will again walk the earth.
Let the cursed monster feel the agony. Let him feel the despair that torments me now.
'My anger was answered by a loud and fiendish laugh. I felt as if all hell surrounded me with mockery and laughter.'
HA! HA HA HA

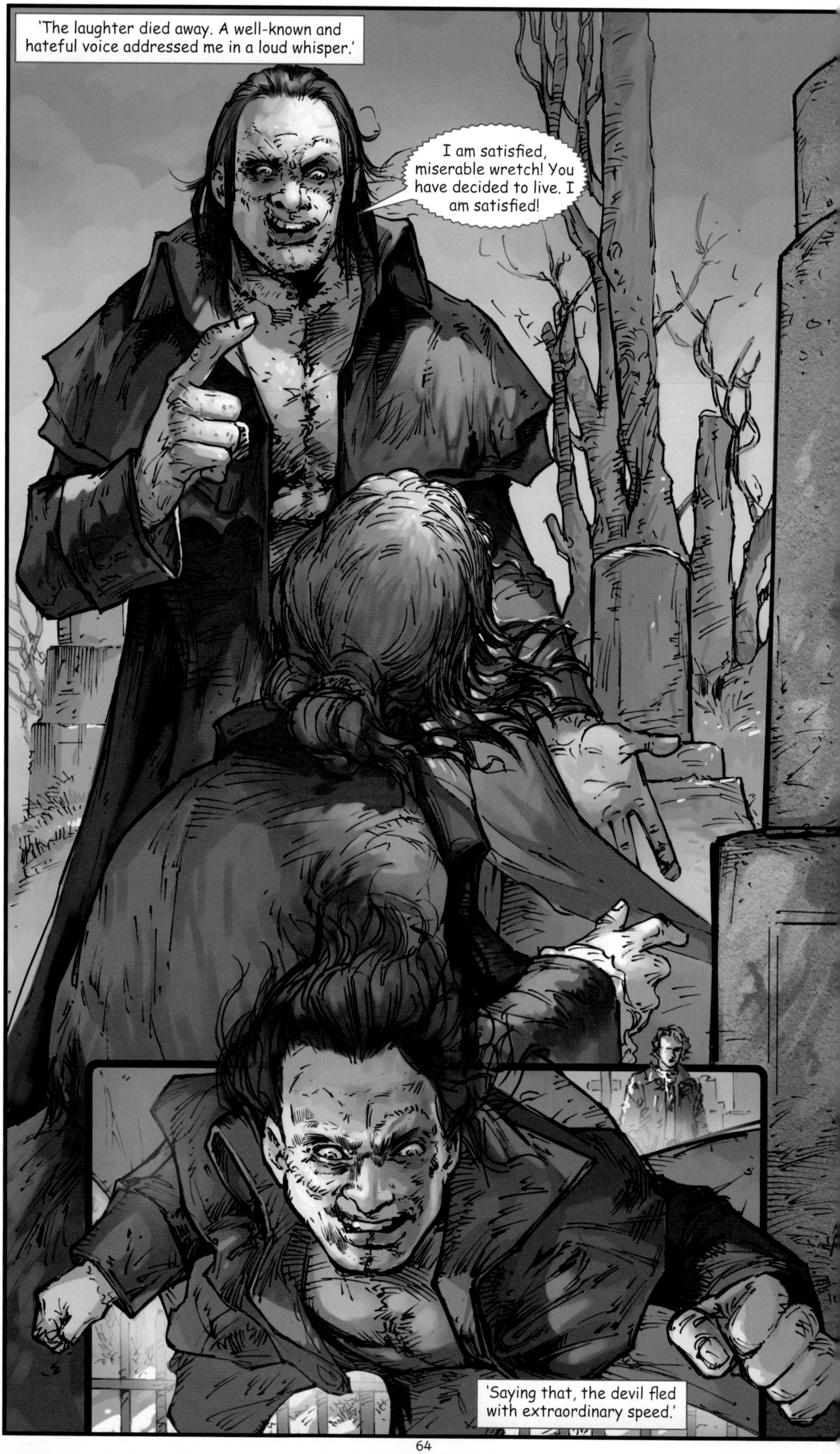
'The laughter died away. A well-known and hateful voice addressed me in a loud whisper.'
I am satisfied, miserable wretch! You have decided to live. I am satisfied!
'Saying that, the devil fled with extraordinary speed.'

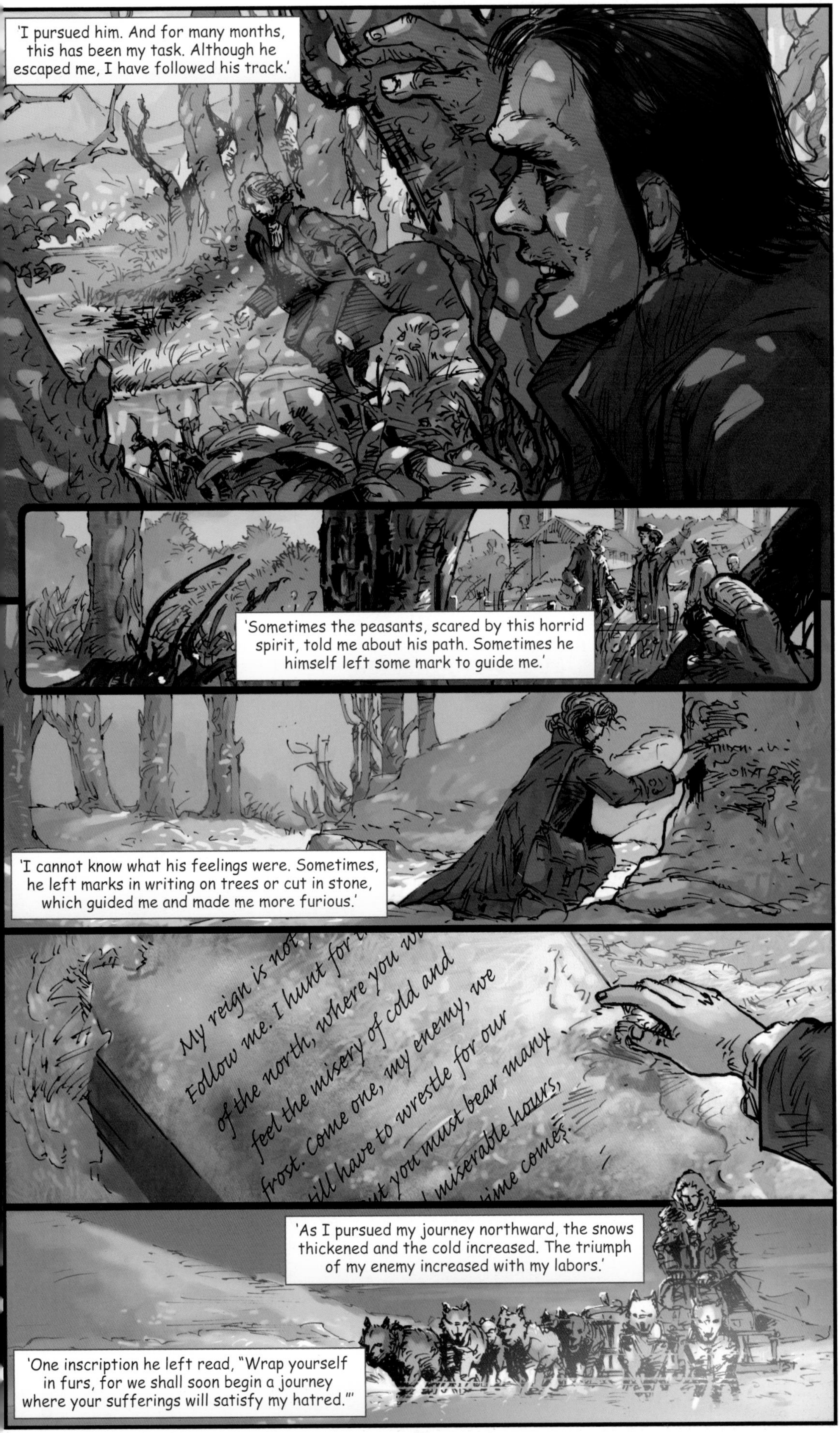
'I pursued him. And for many months, this has been my task. Although he escaped me, I have followed his track.'
'Sometimes the peasants, scared by this horrid spirit, told me about his path. Sometimes he himself left some mark to guide me.'
'I cannot know what his feelings were. Sometimes, he left marks in writing on trees or cut in stone, which guided me and made me more furious.'
My reign is not
Follow me. I hunt for
of the north, where you
feel the misery of cold and
frost. Come one, my enemy, we
have to wrestle for our
you must bear many
miserable hours,
time comes.
'As I pursued my journey northward, the snows thickened and the cold increased. The triumph of my enemy increased with my labors.'
'One inscription he left read, "Wrap yourself in furs, for we shall soon begin a journey where your sufferings will satisfy my hatred."'

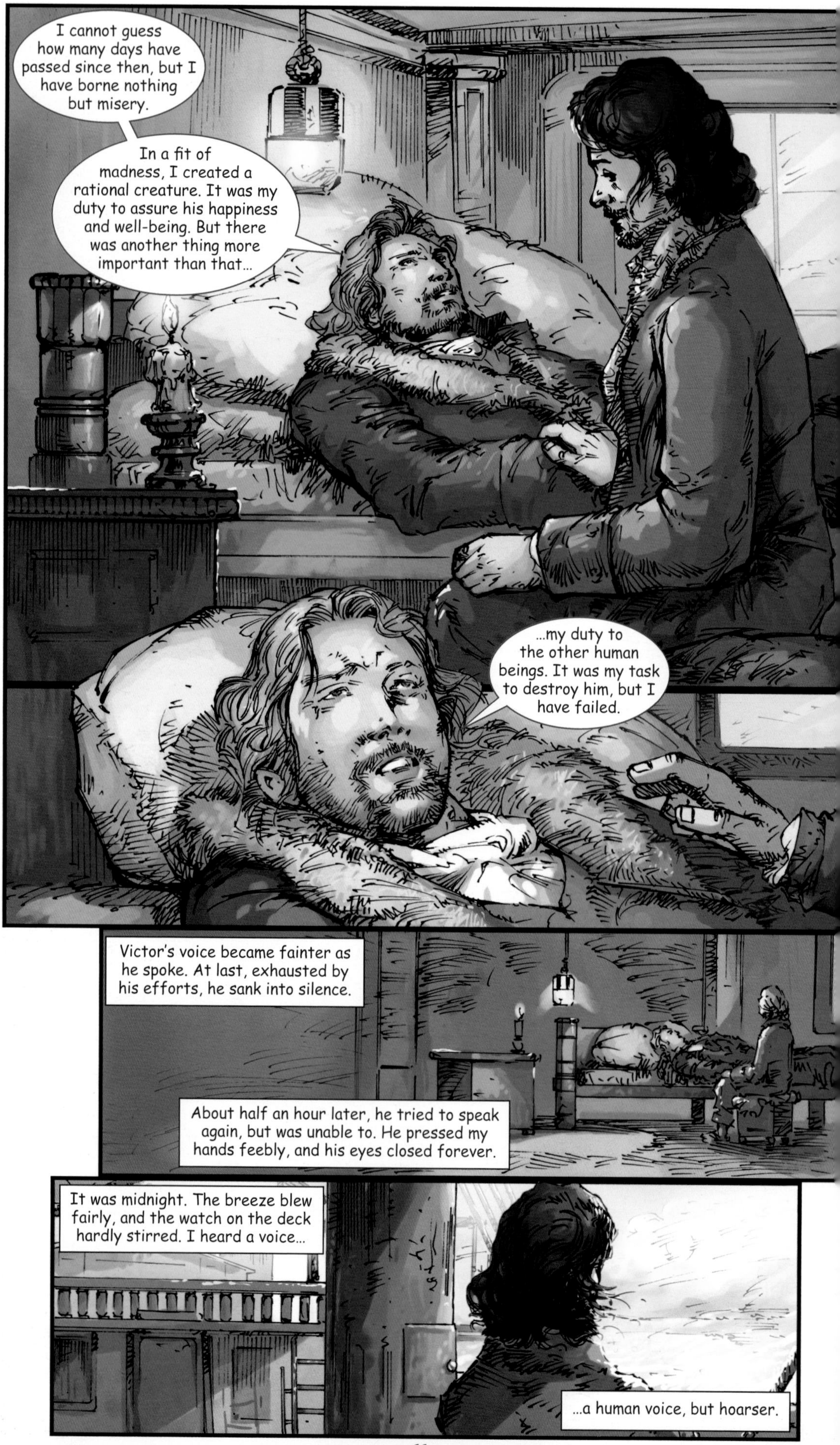
I cannot guess how many days have passed since then, but I have borne nothing but misery.
In a fit of madness, I created a rational creature. It was my duty to assure his happiness and well-being. But there was another thing more important than that...
...my duty to the other human beings. It was my task to destroy him, but I have failed.
Victor's voice became fainter as he spoke. At last, exhausted by his efforts, he sank into silence.
About half an hour later, he tried to speak again, but was unable to. He pressed my hands feebly, and his eyes closed forever.
It was midnight. The breeze blew fairly, and the watch on the deck hardly stirred. I heard a voice...
...a human voice, but hoarser.

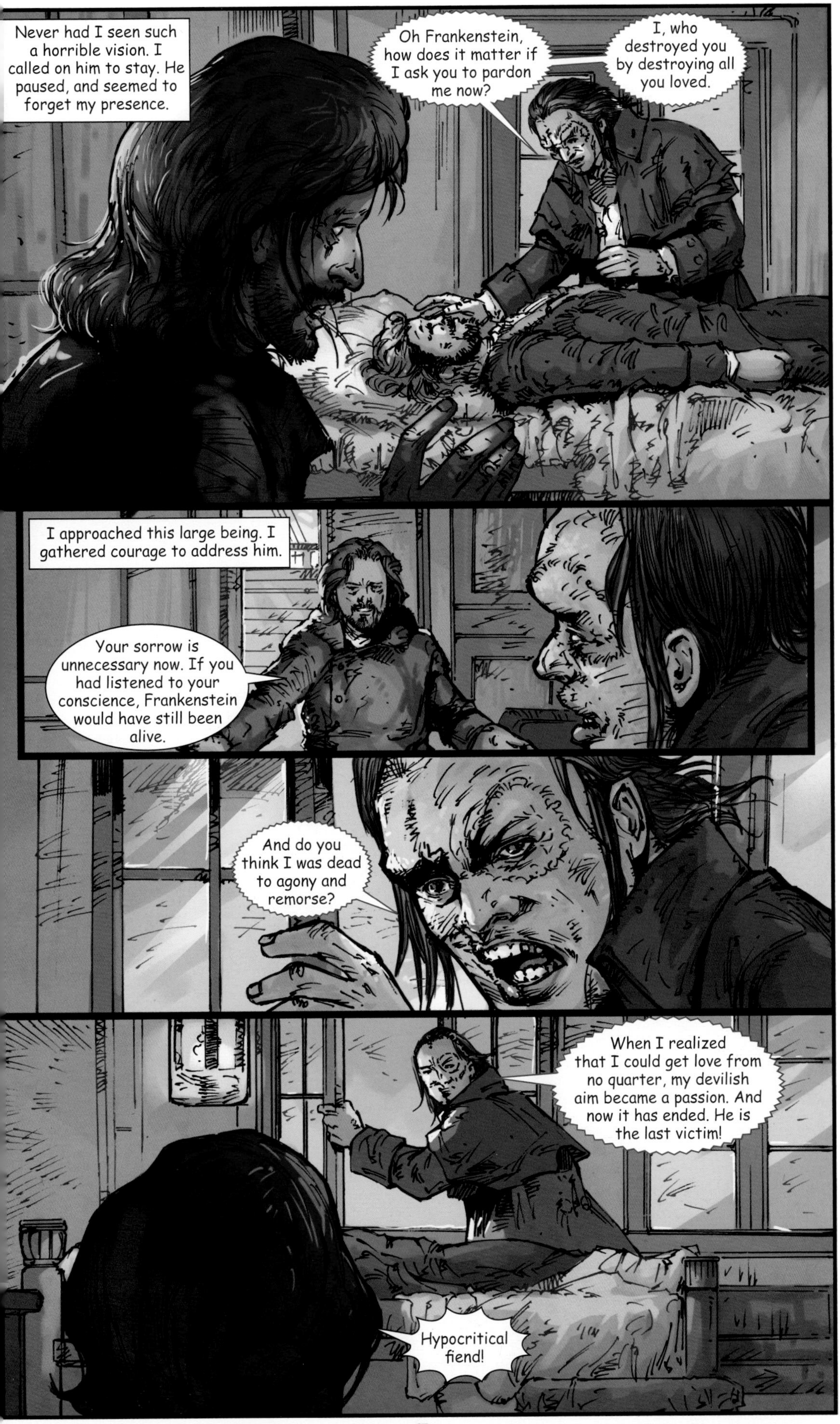
Never had I seen such a horrible vision. I called on him to stay. He paused, and seemed to forget my presence.
Oh Frankenstein, how does it matter if I ask you to pardon me now?
I, who destroyed you by destroying all you loved.
I approached this large being. I gathered courage to address him.
Your sorrow is unnecessary now. If you had listened to your conscience, Frankenstein would have still been alive.
And do you think I was dead to agony and remorse?
When I realized that I could get love from no quarter, my devilish aim became a passion. And now it has ended. He is the last victim!
Hypocritical fiend!

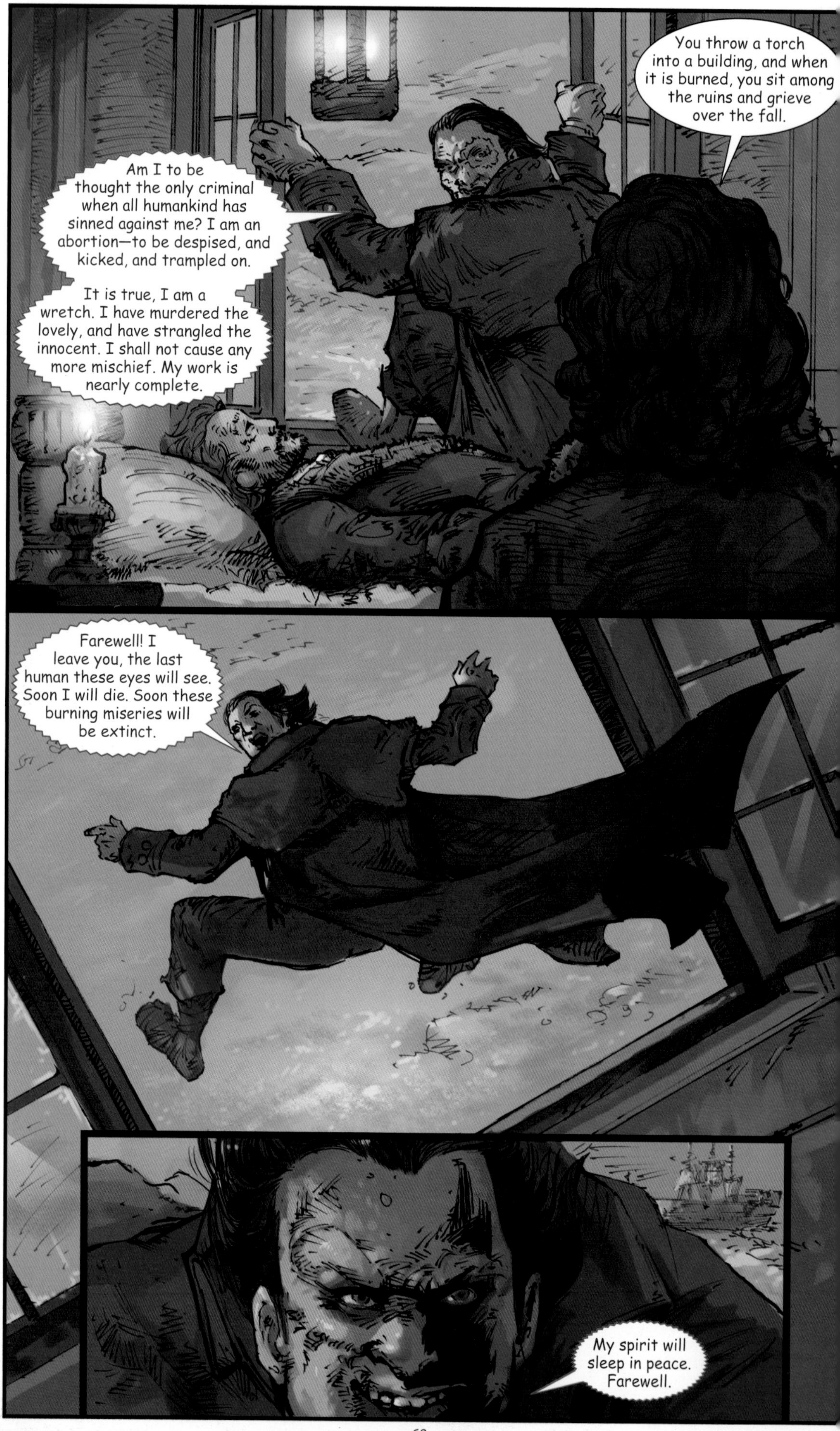
You throw a torch into a building, and when it is burned, you sit among the ruins and grieve over the fall.
Am I to be thought the only criminal when all humankind has sinned against me? I am an abortion—to be despised, and kicked, and trampled on.
It is true, I am a wretch. I have murdered the lovely, and have strangled the innocent. I shall not cause any more mischief. My work is nearly complete.
Farewell! I leave you, the last human these eyes will see. Soon I will die. Soon these burning miseries will be extinct.
My spirit will sleep in peace. Farewell.

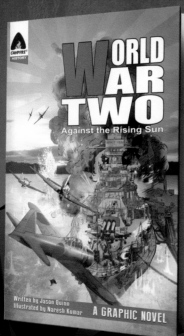

CRYPT CAPERS

In the 19th century in England, the period when *Frankenstein* was published, there were great advances in medical science. Many men like Victor Frankenstein were deeply interested in the human body, and soon anatomy schools and dissecting rooms as a way of learning about the human body had almost become a necessity!

What was body-snatching?

In the simplest of terms, body snatching was the stealing of dead bodies from graveyards. This gruesome act was greatly feared and brought grief to relatives and friends. Freshly buried bodies were taken out of the graves at night and were secretly given to anatomy schools which needed the bodies for their experiments and classes.

Why was there an increase in this activity during the 19th century?

As the number of anatomy schools grew, so did the demand for cadavers (dead bodies). One of the main sources of the bodies was executed criminals. But since there were very few criminals executed, the schools were always in need of bodies. So stealing dead bodies from graves became a good way to meet the demand of the schools. In fact, it became a quite a lucrative business as dead bodies became a commodity and began being sold and bought at really high prices!

Who were the 'resurrectionists'?

The anatomists or their students did not steal the bodies themselves, since they were respected men of society. Instead, they paid people to do it for them. These men would enter a cemetery at night, dig up a recently buried body, and secretly sell it to the local medical school. These men were called the 'resurrectionists' as they sort of resurrected the dead!

Who were Hare and Burke?

William Burke and William Hare lived in Edinburgh in the early 19th century. The story goes that a lodger died owing money in Mrs. Hare's boarding house. Burke and Hare decided to sell the body to cover the debt. They realized that this was a great way of making money. And so began the infamous West Port murders. The two murdered more than 15 vagabonds whom they invited into the boarding house. Thankfully, this moneymaking enterprise ended when the last victim, Mary Docherty, was discovered in Burke's house one morning in November 1828.

What were mortsafes?

Rampant body snatching during the early 19th century led to the invention of mortsafes around 1816. These were heavy iron or iron-and-stone devices in many different designs used to protect graves from theft. Often they were complex contraptions with rods and plates, all locked together. They were especially used in graveyards close to medical schools.

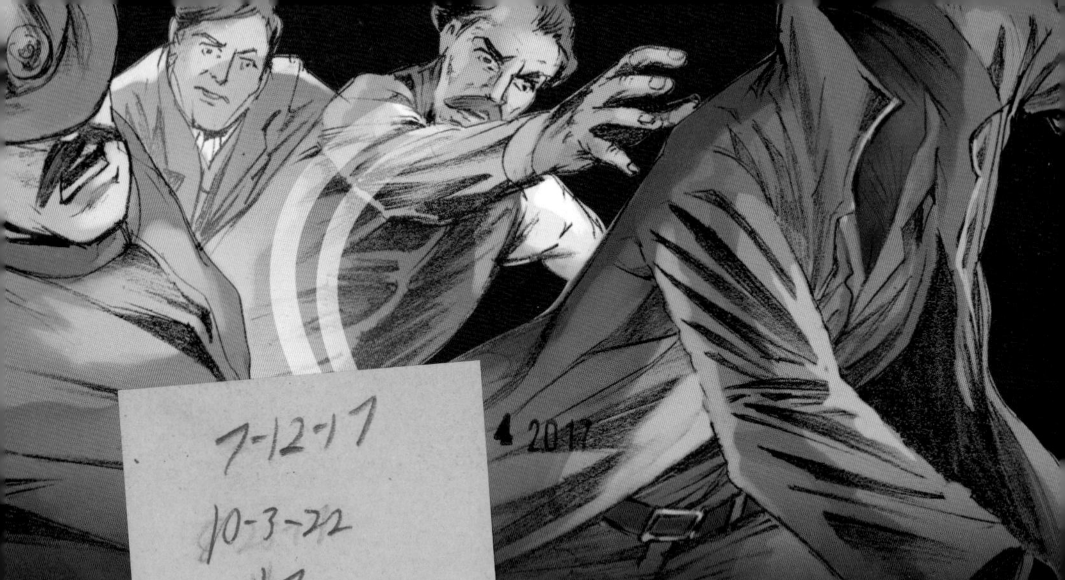

O LIKE TO READ LES FROM OUR CS SERIES

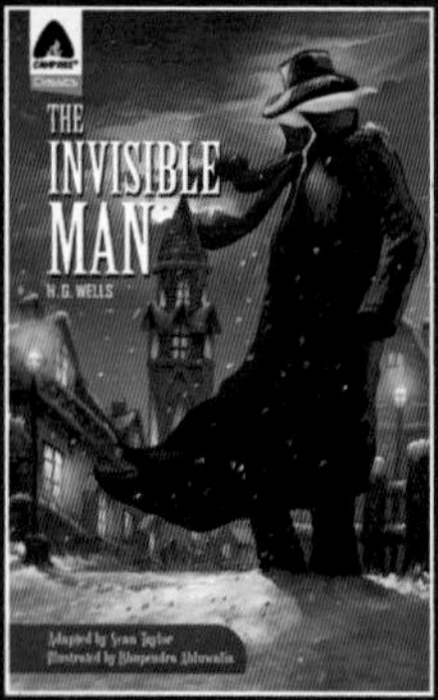
THE
INVISIBLE
MAN
H. G. WELLS

When the residents of Iping first see him, he is wearing an overcoat and goggles, and is covered from head to toe with bandages. They assume he must have been involved in some kind of horrific accident. But as the reality of the situation starts to become clear only one thing is certain—the stranger is a troubled soul and can only deal with his personal fear by terrorizing the people around him. First published in 1897, *The Invisible Man* is HG Wells's warning to the world about the dangers of science without humanity.

Bold visionary Henry Jekyll believes he can use his scientific knowledge to divide a person into two beings—one of pure good and one of pure evil. Working tirelessly in his secret laboratory he eventually succeeds—but only halfway. Instead of separating the good and evil halves, Jekyll manages to isolate only the latter. His friends think Jekyll will waste away and fear the worst. Can Jekyll undo what he has done? Or will it change things forever?

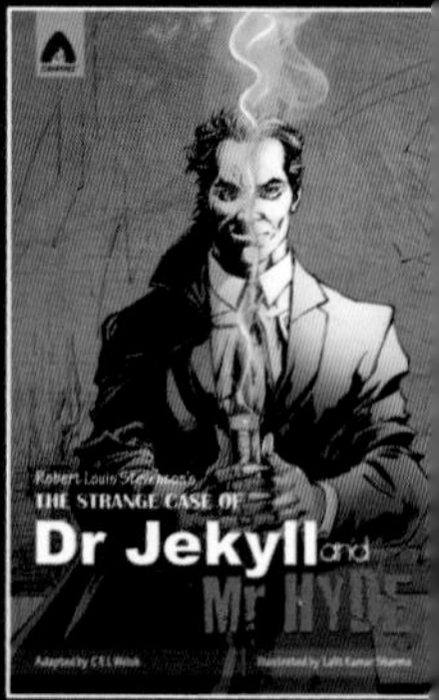
THE STRANGE CASE OF
Dr Jekyll and

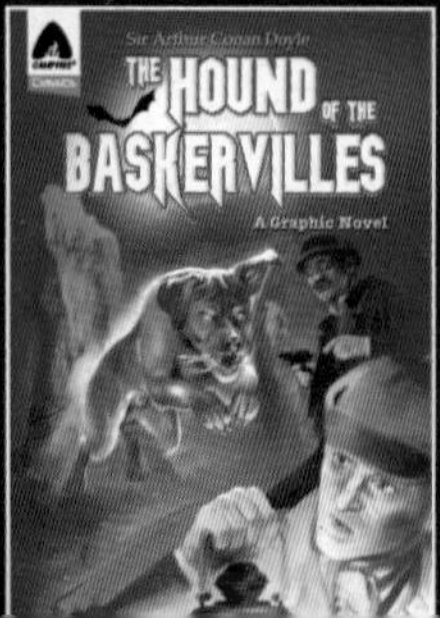
Sir Arthur Conan Doyle
THE HOUND OF THE
BASKERVILLES
A Graphic Novel

When Sir Charles Baskerville is found dead on the moors, a heart attack seems to be the likely cause. However, a certain Dr. Mortimer thinks there is more to it than that. The unparalleled detective Sherlock Holmes, his sidekick Dr. Watson, and an intriguing and mysterious plot make Sir Arthur Conan Doyle's *The Hound of the Baskervilles* a compelling read.